BOOKS BY

SUSAN RICHARDS SHREVE

A WOMAN LIKE THAT (*1977*)

A FORTUNATE MADNESS (*1974*)

A Woman Like That

A Woman Like That

Susan Richards Shreve

New York Atheneum

1977

Library of Congress Cataloging in Publication Data

Shreve, Susan Richards.
    A woman like that.

      I. Title.
PZ4.S5602WO   [PS3569.H74]   813'.5'4   76–50602
ISBN 0–689–10776–5

TO MY MOTHER
HELEN ELIZABETH RICHARDS

TO THE MEMORY OF MY FATHER
ROBERT K. RICHARDS

Contents

I

Emily: *April 1945–April 1956*

Chapter One

MARTIN FIELDING was expected to arrive in Washington on the first of April or thereabouts, the telegram had said. Jane was not enthusiastic. She had agreed, however, at her mother's insistence, to go to Washington a week before the first in case Martin should be shipped out early and to take the child who had not seen her father for three years.

Anthony Call went also. He sat across from Jane and the child, Emily, on the train from Thirtieth Street Station in Philadelphia to Union Station, rode backwards on the harsh woolen seats facing them, his feet crossed between their flanks. Jane Fielding stared stubbornly out the thick window at the Atlantic towns arched grimly against a tedious poverty. She did not speak. Emily watched the way Anthony Call's eyes, half-moon, fell back into his brain and left only the whites showing —milk-cold. It made her feel sick. Her grandfather had told her that Christian children do not hate; nevertheless, she supposed she hated Anthony Call.

But even hating Anthony Call did not pale her excitement at seeing her father. He had been shipped to England four weeks after the Japanese had bombed Pearl Harbor. They had not seen him since. He had written home every day for years (twice a day—one letter to Emily and one to Jane, her mother), until lately.

Lately he had not written home at all, and then the telegram. Emily had been not quite four the winter Martin Fielding left, and the two of them, Jane and Emily, had moved to Tredifferin, her grandparents' farm near Philadelphia, to wait for him. They had not thought it could possibly be so long. Certainly not Jane. She had waited for a while surely, but not since Emily could remember. Emily had waited daily. Keeping his picture on her dresser, his letters under her bed, beneath the rug, so she could read them over and over at night. Once Jane Fielding had come in long after Emily was presumably asleep and found her kissing the gold-framed picture of a serious Martin Fielding from his medical-school yearbook. She had spanked Emily hard.

"You're up long after your bedtime," she had said, but Emily knew there was something more to it.

"Do you suppose his hair is still black?" Emily asked, too nervous not to talk.

"His hair was never black," Jane Fielding replied, annoyed, still staring out the train window.

"But in the picture . . ."

"Pictures always do that." She brushed Anthony Call's feet hard and he woke with a start. "We're almost in Washington, Tony." She said, "His hair was blond. Sandy, just like yours, and I would expect it still is blond."

Once, this year in February, there had been a terrible argument in the dining room next to the study where Emily was sitting with her grandfather, as she often did after school.

"You'll have to break off these petty romances now

that Martin is coming home, Jane," her grandmother had said.

"I won't," Jane Fielding replied, clear as if she had been standing in the same room with Emily. "I waited for Martin for years and I'm tired of waiting."

"That's a woman's place, to wait."

"You never waited, Mother," Jane replied. "You had what you wished from Father in your good time."

"Quiet."

"I like Anthony Call."

"I don't like his family."

"I like him better than Martin."

"You cannot divorce."

"Of course I can. Anyone can and does today. Especially in wartime."

"You are not anyone. You keep up face, and whatever else you do to please your spoiled fancy you do with discretion."

"If I am spoiled, it is you who have spoiled me, Mother." Emily heard a heavy clunk and then a shattering of glass.

When her grandfather opened the door to find out what had happened, Lydia Fowler stood in the middle of the dining room holding the smaller half of a broken plate.

"Your daughter has broken a plate of my grandmother's china."

"I see," he had said, and quietly shut the study door, leaving his wife standing with the broken plate.

It was the first time Emily had sensed the possibility of disaster—the real possibility, since heretofore there had been no arguments amongst them in their years at the Fowlers, only chilly dinners punctuated by the hollow clatter of silver. But no arguments. They were precise, controlled people, the Fowlers, women of narrow emotions who did not give vent to moments of unrefined passions that had not been civilized to manners like glazed pottery generations before. Emily had been at odds with them since she was very small, not consciously, certainly, because she was too young and only knew things were not right in a child's way of sensing wrongness, like the darkness before a storm.

It was a stylized place—Tredifferin—no place for a reckless child at all. Even after the Fowlers lost some money in the Crash, they still maintained Tredifferin from a time when the artifice of order was thought to reflect a civilized mind. The classics bound in leather were on the bookshelves. There was a grand piano in the parlor that no one played. It was no place for this child, except perhaps with her grandfather, who was a simple and rather silly old man—not so old, either, though his brain seemed either very old or very young. He did small, careful things with his life, tended his garden in the morning with infinite patience, and in the afternoon he rocked in the swivel chair behind his empty desk; there was no business to tend to. He loved Emily dearly and she loved him. She did not love her mother. At least not in the ordinary sense. But she was fascinated by her and attracted to her—a base attraction, as though there were with Jane Fielding possibilities for romance. Or evil. Everyone was attracted to her. The parlor at Tredifferin was always full of people, reading in chairs, drinking, talking amongst themselves, or on sofas to themselves or just simply watching Jane Fielding walk amongst them, a high goddess, elegant, distant, cool as darkness, but with a strange capacity to amaze.

"Do you think it's because Mama's pretty?" Emily had asked her grandfather once. "Maybe if she shaved off her hair. She'd look terrible bald. Like a black mole."

Her grandfather shook his head. "They would still come to see your mother even if she shaved off her hair."

"Or her face crumbled in wrinkles?"

"It's not that she's pretty, not at all," he had said. "It's a thing some people have which makes them the center. Other people stick to them as if they were gluey."

"Do you think I will be that way when I grow up?"

"I hope not," her grandfather had replied. "It's a dangerous way to be."

In a primitive sense, Emily understood that danger. She was attracted to her mother but afraid of her too, as if Jane Fielding were capable of destruction.

The train came to a solid stop, throwing Emily against Anthony Call's chest.

"Sorry," she muttered.

"What a clumsy pussy you are." He and Jane laughed.

Always, he called her a clumsy pussy (sometimes he added, without a tail) and always they laughed. It was a clear reason for hating him.

They all got off and walked past the train into the station.

"Do you suppose there's a chance that Daddy might come today?"

"There's no chance," Jane said.

"You don't know that," Emily mumbled. "He could be there when we arrived."

"Absolutely not." Jane hailed a cab and ordered it to the Westchester.

When they arrived at the long, sprawling complex of vaguely grand but very dark brick buildings in northwest Washington, she paid the driver, collected the key and led the way to the apartment they had leased for the duration of their stay. She had remarkable control of situations. It pleased people to watch her as though she were an efficient machine, man-made. Emily followed her at a trot. Behind, arguing with the elevator, Anthony Call struggled with the luggage.

"You can put it in the rooms," Jane said with a flick of her shoulder, striding across the living room, throwing open a window. "Someone must have died here," she said, tossing her coat on the couch. "Or still remains. Anthony, is there a corpse in the bedroom?"

"Where am I sleeping?" Emily asked, following her mother down the narrow corridor to the bedrooms. "With you?" She glanced around for corpses. One could never be sure.

"Alone," Jane Fielding replied. "In here. A lovely pink-damask room fit for an aging widow." She pulled up the shade and let in the afternoon sun.

"Where are you sleeping?" she asked her mother.

"In the other bedroom."

"With Anthony?" Emily asked, surprised at her own boldness, but Anthony had never stayed at Tredifferin.

"Yes, Emily," Jane answered, facing her daughter straight on with her cool gray eyes. "With Anthony."

I I

JANE FIELDING was an astonishingly beautiful woman. People—ordinary people on the street—were struck by her and stopped or whispered as though she carried with her natural elegance a reputation, and people ought to know her on sight.

Until this trip to Washington, Emily had not been to an unfamiliar place with her mother, and she followed through the lobby of the Westchester close on her heels, felt the quiet change Jane Fielding's presence made and was pleased with her relationship to it.

In the mornings while they waited Martin Fielding's return, Emily went down to the lobby to wait for breakfast. It was a busy lobby in the morning, a transient place where people living in Washington for a few months with the War Department or on their way to Europe stayed. Mamie Eisenhower lived there. Several war "widows" had apartments in the Westchester, but hers was the only name Emily recognized. She was a small lady with a warm and confidential smile. One day she stopped and asked Emily how old she was and did she have brothers. She told Emily she had two sons, only one had died. Emily told her about her father, that he was coming home soon and had fought for three years in the war. Then Mamie Eisenhower kissed her and told her how proud she must be of him. Emily hoped Mrs. Eisenhower did not know about Anthony Call.

One day Mrs. Roosevelt came. She ate in the regular dining room with a large group of ladies, but the room was closed off to other guests. Emily could see her, though, simply by sitting up high in one of the chairs in the lobby. Mrs. Roosevelt was eating fruit cup. It amazed Emily that anyone as important as Mrs. Roosevelt would eat fruit cup. Or eat at all.

The fact that Martin Fielding was arriving in Washington on the first of April was confirmed by a second telegram on the thirty-first of March. Jane planned a special dinner with Anthony Call after Emily had gone to bed. But Emily did not go to bed immediately. She sat in the living room with Anthony and watched him pleat the bottom of the Washington *Post*. When Jane came out of the bedroom, her eyes were done dark as caverns; Emily had never seen her mother do her eyes before. She had on a black robe with a split in the center, so when she sat down and crossed her legs, you could see the whole of her slender thighs.

"Very lovely," Anthony said, slipping the newspaper under the chair.

"Have you eaten, Emily?" she asked.

"Yes."

"I think you ought to go to bed early tonight. You have a big day tomorrow."

Emily pushed herself far back into the chair and opened a book.

"At least get in your pajamas."

"When I finish this chapter."

Emily watched her mother slide off her high-heeled shoe, stretch out her leg and rub the woolen knee of Anthony Call with her bare toe.

"Now, Emily," her mother tried again. "It's nearly eight."

"Just a sec." There was something unfamiliar in the

room, like a stranger whom Emily could feel but could not see. It made her uncomfortable, but still she did not leave, as though her presence in that fat stuffed chair were a stay against confusion.

"Emily," her mother said, exasperated.

In bed, with the light off, she could not sleep. She strained to hear voices from the living room but heard nothing except an occasional clink of crystal, so she supposed that finally they were eating. Once, she thought she would get up and tell her mother she could not sleep but thought better of it.

I I I

IT WAS A rare clear day in Washington, when the color of things even at a great distance was absolute. Martin Fielding's hair was white.

They had arrived late at Andrews Air Force Base because Jane had an argument with Anthony after breakfast, so the plane had just landed when they reached the entrance gate—Jane striding cool and lovely as though this day was unremarkable in every sense; Emily perspiring through her new spring coat, nearly sick with anxiety.

When the crew pushed the stairs up to the plane, opened the door, there he was, the first one.

"That's your father," Jane said quietly, without triumph.

Emily strained her eyes. The man, in uniform, Martin Fielding, her father, held the rail and came down the steps with great difficulty, the wind whipping his collar straight back like a brace, whipping his pure white hair.

"But, mama," Emily said, not knowing this shadow of a man. "His hair is white."

"No . . . it's the sun on it," Jane Fielding began, and then, "I suppose you are right. His hair has turned white." She walked out the door, across the field and met him at the bottom of the steps. Emily was close behind her. He embraced them, Jane first, then Emily, with military distance, and did not speak. It was a silent reunion, not at all as Emily had imagined it would be, not like the ones that followed their family reunion, as the jubilant, shrieking families of other soldiers broke the gate and raced to greet the men they had done without. Wordlessly, Martin Fielding stood between Jane and Emily, and the three of them, lit only by an occasional reporter's flash bulb, walked back to the airport, pale, silent specters on the far edge of the joyous crowd. Somehow it had not gone well. Emily wanted to start the day again to make it equal to her expectations.

She rode in the middle between her mother and father. Jane Fielding drove, efficiently weaving in and out of traffic, driving with aggressive certainty, and Martin Fielding leaned back against the seat, a small, tired man with white hair, glad to be driven. Emily didn't know what to say to him.

"You don't seem well, Martin."

"The winter was hard."

"Were you ill? she asked, turning across a bridge into the city.

"I was near a mine blast in December. My leg is still weak."

"You didn't say in your letters."

"It seemed incidental at the time," he said. Occasionally he lifted Emily's hand in both of his and looked at it.

"And lately you haven't written at all."

"I had pneumonia. I got it in February. We were operating half the night, sometimes in bitter cold, and usually to no avail." He picked up one of Emily's braids, flipped it up, strung his fingers through the loose end. "You have my hair," he said, and the corner of his lips twisted into a wry half-smile. "Or the hair I used to have."

There were long silences on the ride back which Jane completed by drumming on the steering wheel or making a strange humming noise in her throat, a swallowed song, which Emily had never heard her do before.

"Did you get my letters?" Martin Fielding asked his daughter. "Do you remember that I used to call you Buffo?"

"I don't remember Buffo."

"I don't know where it came from, but we always called you Buffo from the time you were very small."

"I stopped it, Martin, after you had left. Somehow as she grew older, Buffo seemed to lack dignity. We call her Emily now," she said. "Simply Emily."

"I like Buffo," Emily protested. "Call me that still."

But her father never used the name again.

When they returned to the apartment, Emily checked carefully for Anthony Call (not for Anthony, really, but for a trace, a sock, a handkerchief). She looked in

the bedroom, the closet, under the beds and even in
the sink to see if there was a black circle of bird feathers
midway up the porcelain bowl, which he always left
when he shaved. But Anthony had left without a trace.
It was as if he had never been.

"Anthony has completely gone," she said once to her
mother when they were alone in the kitchen.

"Of course," Jane replied.

The evening did not go well, and Emily was sent to
bed early again, but once at dinner, which he did not
eat, Martin Fielding leaned back in the chair and
watched Jane Fielding with such a look of adulation
Emily nearly choked at sharing in it.

"You are more beautiful than I had remembered,"
he said.

Emily awoke early to a gun-metal dawn without the
sun. She got up and went into the living room just in
her nightgown, without her robe.

Martin Fielding was up, still in his uniform.

"H'lo," she said. "You haven't gone to bed?"

"I couldn't sleep," he answered.

She walked over closer to him. The artificial light
from the lamp haunted his face and he looked very old
to her. Nearly as old as her grandfather, and he was only
thirty-five.

"Sometimes I can't sleep either." She sat down on
the floor next to his long khaki legs, stretched and
crossed in front of him. "Were you surprised to see
me?" she asked. "Did I look different from what you
had remembered?"

"You look different," Martin Fielding replied. "I
would not have known you."

Chapter Two

EMILY WANTED to do bad things. Not simply ordinary bad things that a ten-year-old charged with undirected energy might do—but deplorable things to cause adults to whisper in hushed tones and other children to stand back in cold fear and admiration. She did them too. She smoked black cigarettes behind the kindergarten classroom and talked back when she was caught; she got a D in every course but art and never did her mathematics homework; she had to stay a minute after class for every minute she disturbed the class. For a solid year, she was never home before six o'clock at night. Mrs. Bosnell (smelling thick and sweet as maple sugar, spilling flesh over her own chair and the chair where Emily sat) would sit with Emily, pressing her thin pelvic bone right into the metal, and help her with the math homework from the night before. Or Mrs. Bosnell would do it. When in May Mrs. Bosnell was out for a month with a nervous disorder, everyone said it was plainly caused by Emily, who did not feel a moment of remorse. Once she broke her arm tightrope walking on a high bar on the playground, and another time she walked into the boys' locker room stark naked on a dare.

"I don't like you much," Elsa Sempler said to Emily

one day in art. "No one does, but you're the nerviest girl in all of Friends School."

"Or boy," Emily added solemnly.

She fell in with an unseemly crowd. Archie Boyd, who knocked out both front teeth the week after they grew in (that was the sort of boy he was, bound for self-extinction); Ellsworth Bathes, whose father was Secretary of the Interior in spite of Ellsworth; and Howie, who had no father, or mother for that matter, and lived with his grandparents, who according to Howie drank steadily to forget him. They were all loud and brassy and had reputations. Not Emily. She had a reputation, but she got it quietly. So quietly that it took the headmaster months of seeing Emily after school before he accepted that she was the one involved in the smoking or water bombs or spitballs in the dining room. Until she was caught bare as a wet rat in the boys' locker room and brought straight to his office by the gym teacher wrapped in nothing but a towel.

Then they called her mother.

"I feel certain it's the crowd she spends time with," the headmaster said uncertainly.

"Quite possibly," her mother had answered, and had taken Emily home for her week's dismissal in cold silence.

The Quakers were very patient with her. Not understanding certainly, but patient, practicing that virtue with such gentle insincerity that she wanted to scream and race naked through the whole school shooting a German Luger or pass out Kotex at the lunch table.

The whole thing had started the year before the twins

were born, but it did not really have as much to do with the twins, whom she did not like, as with something else she could not define. Some diminished hope, like the day Martin Fielding had returned from the war.

They had settled in Washington in a large square stucco house in Cleveland Park, and almost immediately Jane Fielding grew fat and sullen with the twins. Martin Fielding started his own practice in family medicine on Eye Street next to Doctors' Hospital and Emily was sent to Sidwell Friends, which was all right for a short time, until things began to fall apart at the center. Soon after Margaret and Charles, the twins, were born, Jane Fielding, as if by one of those German miracles from Grimm, bloomed full and beautiful, a hothouse rose, and was never home. When she was at home, it was as if there were a bright pink boil, thick and ugly, beneath the surface of their lives together and Emily wanted to aggravate it, to cause it to explode. Surely, if you could see it for what it was, it would not seem so ominous as its possibilities. At least that's how she thought about it later. For the moment, all she knew was that she wanted to do wild things of consequence. Like Arthur Kasper, who lived next door. He drove across a ground cable at Fort Myer (in a borrowed car; he was only fourteen) and knocked out the atomic detection system for the whole East Coast. (All of Washington, including a forty-five-mile radius, could have gone up in a puff of radiation, so the general told Arthur's father and Arthur had told Emily.) And Arthur's brother, Jake, who walked along the narrow metal edge of the Calvert Street Bridge (a Washington suicide spot) and fell just beyond the asphalt and did not die. That sort of wild thing of consequence.

Therefore, when Howie suggested the second week of sixth grade that they shoot off cap guns in Quaker Meeting, Emily was all for it. It was, they clearly knew, a thing of consequence to bring a gun—even an innocent facsimile in black plastic—to Quaker Meeting. Only Howie and Emily were left at Friends, anyway. Ellsworth's father had decided to run for the Senate and had gone back to Massachusetts (so he just about had to take Ellsworth), and Archie had been sent to a school for children with mild emotional problems. Howie and Emily had been placed in different sections of the sixth grade. If they were going to shoot off a gun in Meeting, it would have to be the main Meeting on Tuesday that the whole school attended and not simply the Moment of Silence in the classroom.

Emily sat earnest and intent, third row back, a small hard cap pistol stuffed in the wide elastic band of her skirt. Howie was four seats down, in league, and at the appointed moment when one of the teachers stood to shake hands with the teacher sitting next to him, signifying the end of Meeting, Howie shot blat blat blat and Emily followed BLAT BLAT BLAT BLAT.

That afternoon Emily was enrolled at St. Anne's Roman Catholic Convent in Georgetown. It happened that quickly. The Quakers were marvelously efficient when they put their minds to it.

Jane Fielding arrived at two that afternoon to pick Emily up. She had been unavailable in the morning after Meeting and Emily had to wait outside the headmaster's office for hours without even a book to read. Howie's grandfather, cold sober in spite of what Howie had said, arrived half an hour after the shoot-out.

"I get to go to public school," Howie announced triumphantly as he left. It was the last Emily ever saw of him.

Jane Fielding, when she did arrive, seemed not to mind at all. She sat imperious as an eagle, diminishing the headmaster with her cool eyes (beneath a flat hat with a feather that whipped grandly across her forehead).

He fluttered from incident to incident of Emily's fall from grace, cautiously and without conviction, undone by Jane Fielding.

"You're not angry?" Emily asked in the car.

"I'm not surprised," her mother had answered, but absently, as though the last half-hour with the headmaster had impressed a blank film on her mind.

Emily had thought she would be distraught. Had desperately hoped she would.

"St. Anne's will do very well," her mother told her, driving up to the yellow-stucco house and opening the car door for Emily to get out. "I'll be home quite late tonight," she said. "You tell Daddy what has happened."

Cinderella was in the kitchen making supper—beans with fatback, cooking for days. She gave each of the twins a slice of fat, and they sat round and blank as Yo-Yos smacking with ribbons of grease running down their faces. Cinderella was tall—the tallest woman Emily had ever seen. When she stood at the stove, the pans boiled away beneath her hipbone. And she was lovely too, in a strange and foreign way, with a face black as wet bark and eyes so peaceful you would have thought to see her silent, she had reached the promised land—was plain dead. That kind of peace. But you had to see her silent, because talking, she spat fire all around her like some sort of high feathered bird gone cock wild. She worked at the Fieldings because the government didn't hire "colored folks" (the way she said it made it sound like an unpleasant vegetable, stewed), and she had two children to support and she wasn't going to marry some no-good hot-pants black man just to support them because she'd end up supporting him too. (That she told Emily—everything she told Emily, whom she loved.) But she was waiting. She was patient. Her time would come; she was a wise lady.

"Home late as usual," she said as Emily slouched into the kitchen chair.

"Not 'cause of my math," Emily said, pulling her braid out of the girl twin's, Margaret's, solid grip. "I got thrown out."

"Thrown out?"

"I shot a cap gun in Meeting." She threw the pieces of fat Cinderella offered her into the sink. "And the Quakers don't like guns and war and stuff like that."

Cinderella shook her head.

"Well, Howie got thrown out too," she defended. "And he gets to go to public school."

"You haven't got any sense, Emily," Cinderella said, beating the potatoes to white clouds with her long, powerful arms. "A plain child like you ought to mosey along and not cause trouble. One day people's going to take note of you, but don't give them the wrong impression before they even give you a chance."

"It was a dumb school anyway." She took a handful

of cookies. "Now I'm going to a Catholic school. A convent."

"You could use the fear of God a little."

"S'Daddy here?"

"Out in the back with the evening paper."

"I'm supposed to tell him. Also Mother won't be home for dinner tonight. I'm supposed to tell him that too."

"I wouldn't tell him that, sweetheart. He's in bad spirits."

"But she's never home. What news will that be?"

"Just mark what I say. Some things a man don't want to know."

Emily walked out the door and the screen banged behind her.

"Someday there's gonna be more than caps shooting around here," Cinderella said, and sat down on the stool to feed the twins mashed potatoes off the wooden spoon, one blank face at a time.

Martin Fielding was a passionate man with a tightly controlled tendency to excesses. So, he defined himself narrowly within the confines of his science and his parenthood. He was the only son of devout Catholic parents, but he had inherited the passion of their religion and not the God. As with Emily, it satisfied his need for extremes but failed as substance. There was something between him and his first-born child—some recognition of himself in different form that made him at once intensely protective of her and distant. But this afternoon, he was simply strange, abstracted as though part of his mind—the connecting part—had fallen away temporarily. ("It's the war," her mother said when he acted that way. But even Emily knew that was a half-truth.)

"I was expelled from school," she said, sitting down in the flat green-canvas chair across from him, folding her legs beneath her. She expected an outburst or reprimand or to be sent to her room or the basement or somewhere, but nothing happened. He looked up. He looked straight at her, seemed from the intensity in his eyes to be able to see at least four inches beneath her pupils, but he said absolutely nothing at all.

"Daddy." She unfolded her legs and sat straight up. "You see I took this cap gun to school and then shot it at Meeting with Howie. You remember Howie?" He was still looking at her, his newspaper folded in a neat rectangle over his knee, his bright blue eyes leaping out at her beneath his steel glasses—unconnecting.

"You're so quiet," she said in frustration.

"We are both quiet people, Emily," he said finally. "We contain things until there is simply too much to contain any longer and then we explode in a manner often out of our control." He leaned over and took her hand. She squirmed, held her breath to keep from pulling back. He had seldom touched her. "I understand why you shot the cap gun off in Meeting better than you do."

Emily nodded, surprised he understood, for surely there was never a reason as far as she knew why she did any of the things she did. They were just things she *did*.

And then, offhand, as though it hardly mattered, he asked about her mother. "Where'd your mother go after the incident this afternoon" he asked, finishing off the last of his can of beer.

"Gone out." Emily forgot Cinderella's warning. "She said she'll be back late."

"Gone out," he said flatly. He bent the beer can double in his fist; and then with the other hand wrung it so the metal can ripped, and in ripping tore a strip of flesh that bled like running water.

"Goddamn," he muttered, wrapping his hand in a handkerchief he pulled from his pocket.

"I have wanted a family, Emily," he said, "a mother and father and children. A simple thing, you'd think, wouldn't you? In all the years I was in Europe bandaging the superficial wounds of men who'd never heal, it was all I thought about. It was the only thing that seemed to count for something."

He did not come to dinner. Emily ate in the kitchen with Cinderella and the twins.

Later that night, tucking Emily in bed, Cinderella told her about Senator Hallow.

"Now me," she said, patting Emily's thin wrist, "I wouldn't want a man if they dressed him up in church-going clothes and filled his pockets with silver. But some women like your mama need to have a lot of men. Highborn types like this senator. And your daddy just found out about it this afternoon." Cinderella sat with Emily until she fell asleep. "Some men, it takes a long time." From time to time she'd say, almost hum it like a song, "Be easy on your daddy, sweetheart. Be easy."

I I

EMILY KNEW Mrs. Hallow, the delicate, gentle Southern lady with a wide turned-out face, vaguely wilted, just beyond bloom, that Senator Hallow had married. Their son, Douglas, had been in her class at Friends. No intimate surely. The undefiled soul of good, he had not even known her name. But Emily knew him, saw Mrs. Hallow bringing him to school every morning with his rubbers, and they would have a soft argument on the Grayson House steps on whether it might rain. (Emily never wore rubbers. She'd stuffed hers behind the gym lockers, which wouldn't be cleaned until spring.)

Once in Garfinkel's, after Emily knew about her mother and Senator Hallow, she saw Mrs. Hallow again. Jane Fielding was buying slips. She had at least twenty-six of them in different sizes spread rainbow on the counter top, and Emily, sitting on the thick, fat carpet, her back against the showcase, watched her mother through the glass. Suddenly looming double and distorted in the pastel slip glass was Mrs. Hallow in shambles. Her blouse, bunched up under her suit, her face rough and pale as squash.

By this time, Jane Fielding was brazenly going off weekends with the senator, although she would say for Emily's sake that she was going off to visit Aunt Kay or to the ballet in New York. But Emily knew better.

"Hello, Eleanor," Jane Fielding said, as if it was the most natural thing in the world for them to be buying underclothes together.

"I must buy something," Eleanor Hallow said meekly, as though it would be quite agreeable if the clerk would just bag anything in the store. "Jim is running again this year . . ." She sorted through the slips haphazardly without interest. "I haven't bought a thing in six years. Not since his last campaign."

"Jim tells me this will be a difficult race."

"So I understand."

"Some new young man who's made a reputation for himself in North Carolina is his opponent."

"Maybe I should get some slips," Mrs. Hallow said absently.

"Well, it should be exciting."

"Or a nightgown. I do need a nightgown."

And, boldly, Jane Fielding pulled a negligee off the hanger—a bare slice of pale silk—and held it up to herself, letting it fall over that slender jewel of a body.

"Oh, I don't think so." Mrs. Hallow paled. "It's . . . oh, I don't know."

"Do you like it, Emily?" Emily ground her head into the circle of her arms. Her mother could surprise her still.

"Perhaps I need a suit." Mrs. Hallow wandered off beyond them and Emily saw her as she left, circling the round swings full of suits, fingering the material, moving vacantly to another counter.

"I ought to get it, then," Jane Fielding said. "I'm completely out of gowns."

She could be a terrible woman, and the fearsome thing was that it was neither intentional nor vindictive. It was inherent and without remorse.

Martin Fielding took to falling asleep on the living room rug. It was not drinking (which is what most people suspected), but an overwhelming tiredness which overtook him. Many times Emily would find him there after dinner and try to wake him unsuccessfully. For a time, she decided he had a terminal sleeping disease and began to sit by his bed at night, certain he would slip away from her; he was never conscious of it. Jane

Fielding was seldom home after dinner, often did not come in until the middle of the night. Her car in the driveway would waken Emily, and, awake, she would stiffen, listen for the muffled steps on the stairs, the door to her parents' room, and in some space between would fall back to troubled sleep. Once, Emily asked her father why he did not leave, simply take her (it never occurred to her to include the twins) and leave Jane Fielding without a word. He looked astonished, as though she'd spoken sacrilege.

"I never would," he said. "At least not now."

One night, a bleak winter night when unrelenting rain had turned the city to a swamp, a frantic Martin Fielding delayed dinner two hours, certain that Jane would be home.

"She's not coming home, Dr. Fielding," Cinderella said emphatically.

"She's been in an accident," he insisted. "She *said* she'd be here."

"She's been confused about the time we eat around here more than once." Cinderella stormed into the kitchen and served a plate to Emily. "Thinks we have dinner at four A.M."

"It's got to be something. She talked to me at five— just before I left the office." He called the police, checked the hospitals for any accidents, the Arena theatre, where she danced, a friend she knew at Dupont Circle, and then the hospitals again.

"Won't you have something?" Cinderella asked. "Pretty soon this food's going to dry up and disappear."

"I'm waiting for Jane."

When Emily went in, Martin Fielding was asleep on the living room rug. She sat on the chair beside him reading *True Romance* behind her history book so Cinderella wouldn't catch her. It was lately her only sin—she would read with earnest delight "I Loved My Sister's Boyfriend," or "I Ran Off with My Daddy and Left My Mama Crying the Blues," and then at night, before she went to bed, she would get on her knees and pray to her Almighty Father to forgive her her sins. She had settled temporarily with the Roman Catholic God. It was specific and ordered and gave her things to do—prayers to say, uniforms to wear, a simple history (at least in half-truths voiced in catechism) that extended uninterrupted into a dark past and connected her with Jesus on the Cross. She was never much interested in Jesus beyond the Cross or even before, but that young man with nails through his hands gripped her imagination; she needed something that powerful to dispel the general disorder of her own life. She did not believe. She was consumed, and for a brief time, St. Anne's delighted in this wayward child, brought home to the Father, saved from sin.

Jane Fielding did come home that night. She rushed in the front door, ablaze with joy, hair damp and swinging, all askew, cheeks flushed with rain (this fastidious woman who showed only the refinement of emotion, impeccable even in crisis). She rushed over to Martin Fielding (dead asleep on the carpet), took him by the shoulders and woke him with energy.

"Jane," he groaned. "I thought you had been in an accident."

"I was." She cradled his head in her arms. "I would have called you, but it was such a simple accident. No one hurt but the car."

"You're not at all hurt?"

"Not at all." She kissed him. Emily burrowed behind her history book. She had never seen them kiss, and seeing it now (with the distinct flavor of *True Romance*), she thought there was passion. Later, looking back with the knowledge of what happened between her parents, she understood it was frank power that she mistook for passion.

Jane helped Martin to his feet. "I have something wonderful to tell you," she said, and together, wrapped together, they went upstairs. Jane pulling him with her. Enchanting him.

Emily slipped out of the chair, up the back stairs and climbed into bed, but she could not sleep for thinking that Jane Fielding had seen the "truth," that their differences were over (her Catholicism she took for gospel then). Her mother was saved and that was the wonderful thing that had happened to her. Emily slept an empty sleep lulled by a child's remarkable capacity for hope.

The next morning, Jane Fielding left the house at seven with a neat brown bag, dressed from the cover of *Vogue*, a high-fashioned sinner. She was gone all weekend.

Pale and empty, Emily sat across from her father at the breakfast table.

"You ought to leave her," she said solemnly.

"I can't," her father answered.

That woman, that bright-eyed, brazen, beautiful woman who dashed into the house and urged Martin Fielding up to her bed, kissed him and cajoled him, sliding into the pale silk thing she found at Garfinkel's —that woman Martin Fielding simply could not leave. She possessed him, and through all his sleeping on the living room floor, he had the hope that she would rush in the front door and possess him once again.

Chapter Three

SOMETIME BEFORE HER FIFTEENTH BIRTHDAY, Emily
stopped being a Catholic. The rituals of Catholicism had measured and occupied her life with a series of
thoughtless and predictable routines that did not any
longer make sense. She exchanged Catholicism for making love—or thoughts of making love. It seemed an entirely plausible exchange. She dropped everything and
spent most of her time face down on her bed pressing
her lips against the imaginary cotton-quilt lips beneath
her or wrapping around the light post on Thirtieth
Street, pale and lethargic as lank squirrel skin, waiting
for Michael McCarthy (who did not know her—had in
all probability never heard of her) to pass by St. Anne's.
She supposed she was in love with him. If so, it was the
second time she had been in love.

She had been thirteen the first time. Troubled by the
usual shambles of her family's incautious destruction of
each other, confused by an anxious growing thirst in
her groin, she spent hours in the secrecy of her bedroom with thoughts of violent love and violent death.
She was her most Catholic then (she wanted to be consumed by Pentecostal fires—that sort of Catholic), and
the man she fell in love with—for he was a man, a
Catholic priest of nearly fifty with eyes bright as candles
—became the receptacle for her life. She put herself to

sleep at night with his face impressed like an indelible woodcut on her brain. He called her Sarah, confusing her with Sarah Huston, who was as bland and passionless as a blown dandelion. Unable to make herself known to him, she wrote him a note and left it in his school mailbox, sealed—

I AM IN DESPERATE NEED OF HELP OR I WILL KILL MYSELF.   SARAH.

Mother Superior called her into the office the following morning at eight o'clock sharp, straight after Mass.

"I am not Sarah," she defended. "I didn't write the note."

Father James came in and sat across from her, his eyes blazing.

"We asked Sarah Huston," Mother Marie Joseph said, "and Father James tells me he has confused you with Sarah in the past."

He nodded, his eyes approaching awkward benevolence. "I am sorry, Emily," he said apologetically.

Emily was mortified, sitting in the stuffy wooden room with the giant God-infested black blimp leaning over her smelling of sweet soap, and the man she loved sitting distant as a mountain range across from her.

Of course he knew, she thought—had probably told Mother Superior that it had happened once before in New Jersey with a girl quite like Sarah—rather, Emily —and he'd said three extra Hail Marys for any part he might have had in it. But this would pass, he had assured her. Girls can be quite capricious, he had noticed.

They questioned and cajoled her, upbraided her gently but with the distance of formal religion, and finally delivered a lecture about the sin of taking one's own life (even talking about it in jest) that lasted beyond milk and crackers, well into math class (all the while she was thinking of climbing to the top of the Georgetown tower and flinging herself onto the ground, landing about the same place where Father James would pass to go to Mass. See what three Hail Marys would do for him then!).

"It wasn't me who wrote that note," she insisted, and knew they did not believe her.

Then Father James went out of his way, sought her after Mass, in English class, before sports, to say, "Hello, *Emily*." She hid in the girls' room if she saw him coming. It was sometime after Father James that she stopped being a Catholic. It was not substantial and Father James was not to blame—simply a convenient cutting-off point. Only the form had mattered—the novenas, the stations of the cross, uniforms, saints' days, good works and prayers—a daily way to be which she could easily learn and which appealed sufficiently to a growing sensuality, yet kept it intact. The form of Catholicism took time and energy, however; now Emily had too much time. She was on academic probation, and though she had been on academic probation off and on for years, it took on a new complexity, just as everything had without the simple truths of the past but with air pockets of confusion in their place.

"Trouble is," Cinderella told her one afternoon, "comes a time when a girl gets needful, and your time has come."

"Needful of what?" Emily asked, eating the freshly shelled peas.

Cinderella gave one of her broad twisted shrugs that

said more in body than ever was said in words.

"A man!" Then she laughed loud and long, just threw her head back and rang bells in the kitchen. "A nice, slim, good-looking, no-count man." She cleared her throat. "Or something better."

"Like what?"

"Like the love of God, sweetheart."

She shook the peas in the colander like cymbals. "Time was when I thought you'd manage fine. Time was . . ."

"I'll manage fine," Emily said. "I'm going to cut off my braids."

"Sounds like you're up to no good."

"Don't worry, Cindy. Mama's found all the no-count men around. There's no one left for you and me."

"Hard work." She shook the peas into a pot of boiling water. "Plenty of hard work and a little laughter. That's what's left to the likes of you and me." Then she cocked her head and gave Emily a curious and unfamiliar look. "I suppose you know about your father's mice."

"Mice?"

"Mice," she replied. "He keeps mice in his office."

"I know he's doing a cancer experiment," Emily said. "That's where he is on Saturday mornings."

"And Saturday night and Sunday. At first I thought his mice had two long legs and soft round bowls right here." She strutted like a hen, pressing her breasts. "I thought to myself, Bless my soul, this man is going to give Mrs. Jane Fielding back a little of the medicine she's given him for all these years. But this morning I was at his office to have my annual heart checkup and there they were in the back room—one glass box after the next just full to flooding of those little brown furry things." She leaned back against the stove, wiped her long slender hands on her apron and folded her arms across her chest. "It almost broke my heart."

Emily slid onto the chair. "What d'you mean?"

"He's not going to find out anything about cancer in mice." She shook her head. "He doesn't even want to."

"He doesn't?"

"He doesn't," she said absolutely. "He's given up, sweetheart." Cinderella unbraided Emily's hair. "Plain given up."

Emily sensed the strong compassion in the older woman as she stroked her long hair with iron hands, but she did not understand what she had done to awaken it.

Emily would not go to Mass. Sister Marie Joseph said, "When in Rome do as the Romans do." Emily replied she was not in Rome, so she had to go to Saturday detention for insolence. The night before detention, she spent the night at Jane O'Reilly's, drank bourbon straight from the O'Reillys' liquor cabinet, and though Jane O'Reilly, who did the same thing, threw up all night and finally fell asleep on the bathroom floor, Emily arrived at St. Anne's the next morning boldly drunk without having slept a bit all night. Sister Marie Joseph called her father, who came to get her right away. On the way home, he had to stop the car right on Wisconsin Avenue in the middle of traffic because Emily was sick.

"I'm sorry, Daddy," she said numbly.

"We should've taught you to drink. Had you sit down at the table with us and have a glass of wine," he said quietly. "If we had an ordinary family, that's what we should have done. It's how I learned."

"It's not your fault, Daddy," she insisted, but there was no telling him anything—his mind slid away so quickly. So he took her home, gave her tomato juice, told her to sleep and went back to his office to work with his mice.

The boarders at St. Anne's took baths in nightgowns or powdered water so they wouldn't see themselves and be tempted. Nevertheless, they were tempted and thought of nothing else; but they were afraid. Emily was afraid too, though not sufficiently. She wanted something overwhelming to happen to her equal to the chaos in her own house, in her own mind, so she decided to lose her virginity—quite matter-of-factly, as if it were a thing, a tangible possession of which one quite handily and in reasonable mind disposed. It was not easy. Someday, she would be a handsome woman with fine bones, but for the moment, she was simply long—too long for any boy she knew. Arthur Kasper, who lived next door, was out of the question, although she'd had two rolls of colored pictures taken of Arthur with her (Emily in evening dress, Emily in bathing suit, Emily in short shorts, Arthur always in blue jeans) just to have something in her wallet besides school pictures of the twins whom she still despised. She finally got Jane O'Reilly's brother Pete to kiss her at a party at the O'Reillys', but he went home with Peggy Southern and that was that. But when Andrea Piget had her sixteenth birthday party, Emily left early with Tommy Stealer, who was a turkey, everyone solemnly agreed, but one had to start somewhere and Emily had known Tommy all her life. It was therefore a great surprise to him (after they'd parked on the Cathedral grounds at her suggestion, to talk about things, and he kissed her because she was nearly sitting on the steering wheel) that she took off her coat, her sweater and her bra and sat in the front seat naked from the waist up.

"Listen, Emily." He turned on the engine of his car. Then the radio full blast. "Listen. I mean."

"What do you mean?"

"I mean, you know." He lit a cigarette and breathed so much in that he choked. "You better put your coat on." He drove down past the College of Preachers, past the dean's house, onto Woodley Road. Emily put on her coat.

"I just simply couldn't," Tommy said, driving up in front of her house. "I mean, I really like you. You're a neat girl and all."

Emily jumped out of the car and rushed up the front stairs of her house carrying her sweater and bra. "Oh, shut up," she said to no one in particular.

About this time, Emily won a national prize for high school artists for a painting she had done in art class.

"I simply knew there was something there," Sister Anne Donnelly told Sister Marie Joseph, "some quality worth saving, worth discovering."

"It will be a jewel in your crown in heaven, Sister, that you have touched on what the rest of us have missed in Emily," Sister Marie Joseph said.

The winning painting was displayed in the Corcoran Art Gallery along with all the runners-up from other states. St. Anne's all went on chartered buses to see it and got to miss the four periods after Mass. Tommy Stealer had second thoughts and asked Emily to a movie when he read about her on the second page of the *Post,* and Sister Marie Joseph had her to tea in her own private quarters and told her, "God helps those who help themselves," and *Parade* magazine did an article on the whole Fielding family.

Emily sat at the kitchen table with Cinderella, reading the story. There was a picture of the family on the front page, a color picture neatly arranged with Emily in the middle in her uniform, looking like a telephone pole with feet, Jane Fielding (back from a two-week trip to Jamaica where she had met another man, although she went with Senator Hallow), looking exquisite, taking over the picture as if she were painted silver, an aged Martin Fielding, standing behind the love seat in the hall, blinded by the photographer's light, and the twins in navy blue, side by side, grown simply rounder, blanker, duller by the year like cardboard models of themselves. The article described the Fieldings as an average advantaged middle-class family with a talented daughter who would "go someplace."

"An average middle-class family," Emily read aloud to Cinderella, who was polishing silver. "Listen to this, Cindy. 'Dr. Fielding has a thriving practice in family medicine—his wife, a lovely, dark-haired lady, is involved with the Arena Theatre as a dancer, with the American Cancer Society and of course with her children. . . .' "

"Of course." Emily put her feet on the kitchen table, spread the magazine out on her stomach. "Mother hasn't even stopped to notice whether she still has children."

But Emily was wrong. Jane Fielding was quite aware of children. She was pregnant. Throughout that long winter, Emily watched with fascination as the lithe body thickened, simply thickened as if there were a perfectly round doughnut tied about her middle.

"D'you think it's on purpose?" Emily asked Cinderella, impervious to the twins, who were delicately eating an afternoon snack, sitting upright, bright red stuffed olives.

"She said she wanted four children." Cinderella shrugged. "Just the other day, she came into the kitchen, just swung on in here, dressed in her robe, and the Lord knows, I've never seen her in a robe before, and said to me—I must have looked a little disbelieving—'Four is a perfect number, Cindy, and we hope it is a boy.' "

"Jesus." Emily burrowed her head in her hands. "Well, it's encouraging to know she can count the ones she already has."

"Your hair's on the table," Margaret screeched at Emily.

"D'you think it's hers, Cinderella?" Emily asked, ignoring her sister, moving in fact a little closer to be certain that her hair was on the table.

"Now, Emily"—Cinderella raised her eyebrows—"surely you can tell with your very own eyes. If it's growing in her belly, it must be hers."

"Theirs. You know what I mean."

"You hair's getting on my graham crackers," Margaret wailed.

"Many things your mama is," Cinderella said, moving Emily's head away from Margaret, "stupid is not one of them."

Jane Fielding stayed home. She went to parent conferences, PTA meetings, served on committees for bazaars, took Margaret to dancing lessons and Charles to flute lessons and Emily to Saturday-morning detentions and Thursday-afternoon extra math classes. She stayed home at dinnertime and invited Emily to have a drink of wine in the library with her parents before dinner so the same thing wouldn't happen at Jane O'Reilly's again, and did needlepoint in the living room after dinner, talked to Martin Fielding about Max Acton's ulcers and Tom Jenkins' liver problem and whether the Bateses were adjusting to the death of their youngest daughter. They went to Cuba for two weeks in February, and when they returned, dark as prunes, Martin Fielding looked less than sixty for the first time Emily could remember. He had stopped sleeping on the living room rug, had forgotten his glass cages full of mice at various stages of degeneration and came home every night early half-believing Jane Fielding would be gone. But she was there running the kitchen that Cinderella had run with absolutely no help for eight years.

"Let's have mushrooms with some thyme over the beans tonight, Cindy," she'd say, "and the beans not so dreadfully overdone."

"We haven't got mushrooms," Cinderella would reply sourly.

"Then run off to the Giant and get some," Jane would say. "In Europe women shop every day."

"This isn't Europe," Cinderella would mumble under her breath. But off she would go to the Giant for mushrooms.

Jane Fielding took Emily to Mass every Sunday even

though it was Martin who was the Catholic. She talked to Sister Marie Joseph three times about Emily's grades and agreed that Emily should probably go to Rosemont College, a pleasant Catholic girls' school in Philadelphia, because she had seeds of recklessness that would certainly be sown if she went straight to art school.

(Emily did the best she could in the back seat of Tommy Stealer's car, after he had reconsidered and taken her out, but even so the car was built all wrong, and once Tommy, who was very nervous and impatient by nature, got her on her back on the floor of the back seat, there was a great hump on the floor and Tommy bumped his head on the metal ashtray trying to get in the right position; it simply didn't work out at all and, to make matters worse, the Cathedral police shone the high beams on them, so Tommy took her home and told her they just didn't seem to be suited to each other except as good friends.)

After years of freedom from parental care, Emily was overwhelmed by her mother's transformation. She flunked everything, wasn't allowed to take art, wrote a poem about making love for English class and had to see Father Joseph twice a week about saving herself for her husband, which it looked like she was going to have to do in spite of her efforts to the contrary.

The yellow house in Cleveland Park had become very ordinary and calm—almost normal—for the first time in Emily's memory. But it was an ominous calm like the moment in the center of a hurricane before the devastation. Emily knew it. It gave her a sense of cold terror such as she had never known in the years of her mother's philanderings. Martin knew it too—he was straight-bristled, on edge, like a desert fox alert to wind change.

"I'm just hopeful there'll be no need to have pimentos on the green peas tonight because there's no pimentos in the house and I'm not anticipating walking through that snowstorm for a jar of pimentos or a box of mushrooms."

Emily laughed. "It's weird, isn't it?"

Cinderella shrugged.

"D'you think it's permanent? Like maybe she's just going to be different from now on. She knitted a sweater today. C'n you imagine?"

"I can imagine," Cinderella said. "But wild birds are wild birds. I know that too."

I I

ON SUNDAY evenings, the Fieldings went to the Chevy Chase Club for supper and took Emily. After dinner there was dancing. All the children, dressed to the nines, looking absurd, not like children at all but Best and Company monsters, would dance first (their parents at the tables around the dance floor, proud as punch that their re-created images could do a bite-size two-step like stiff-armed, white-patent-leathered adults). Emily did not dance. Her legs were as long as most of the bodies and still, at sixteen, she had not grown into them. She would slink into the depths of her chair in the corner of the dance floor and look miserable. She wore her uniform, the only thing she felt vaguely human in, and pinned her hair up in a chaste knot at the back of her head.

The end of the calm came one Sunday evening at the Chevy Chase Club.

There was a new man at the dance that evening—not a handsome man, but striking with command. Everyone had noticed him, even Emily. When he danced, he controlled the dance floor as if the orchestra played for him alone.

"Martin." Jane Fielding looked over. "Do you know that man?"

"I've never seen him," Martin replied, with an edge.

The man danced by the table, and even in that short space, there was an exchange between him and Jane Fielding, a chemical exchange that Martin Fielding, attuned for years to that kind of thing, understood.

"We ought to leave now," he said, finishing his drink in a rush. But it was too late; the man was there asking Martin if he could dance with Martin's wife.

"Mind?" Jane slipped back at Martin.

He shook his head, ordered another drink with water, but drank it straight from the small shot glass without the water and then ordered another.

"I thought we were going," Emily said from the corner of her chair.

"We were," her father replied.

Jane Fielding and the man danced through several selections with such grace that people at the tables noticed and other people on the sidelines or the dance floor sat back down at their tables. They were the only people left on the dance floor when the band played a tango, the last tune before their break. Hip to hip they were, the unborn child spread between them just barely stretching the straight dress Jane wore, their faces bright, in tune, glowing with their shared cockiness as they slid across the floor. There was no question even to Emily of what was going on.

The Fieldings left when Jane came back to the table. Silently Martin gripped her elbow and Emily's and strode to the car.

"You are hopeless, Martin," Jane said, shaking her mass of black hair and climbing into the car.

Martin drove as fast as he had ever driven in his life. The protected corner of his brain overtook him and he raced down Connecticut Avenue through two red lights, careening around Chevy Chase Circle, the car's side nearly parallel to the road on two wheels, or so it sounded, there was such a tear of rubber. He had to stop or cross the grass center strip of the circle and the police picked him up there. He was pressed between the two officers in the front seat, Emily and Jane in the back seat behind him.

Jane Fielding was a model lady. She stood lovely at his side, smiled vaguely at the police chief, who couldn't keep his sluggish eyes off her. She was admirably forbearing and controlled while Martin was ticketed and they were all driven back to Chevy Chase Circle.

"I'll drive," she said to the officer, climbing into the driver's seat. She reached across the front seat and opened the door for Martin.

"I would, lady," the officer replied and shook his head.

Martin Fielding got into the front seat next to her,

his body electric, so taut that Emily could feel it in the back seat, where she had concealed herself.

"Bloody bitch," he said with vehemence.

Jane Fielding sat in the library chair the next few months and waited for the baby (who was a girl called Jillian) to grow, her belly puffing slowly, blown from within with hot air. And then, in the space of a few hours, Jillian was expelled, passed like a kidney stone with enormous relief. She got up from childbirth as though her body had in fact been filled with nothing more than air, and was off triumphant as a peacock.

She danced at the Arena Theatre (once she was offered a part in a movie and turned it down, but she was quite good) and went to lunches and dinners and parties sometimes written up in the *Post,* often with Senator Hallow, who said they were extremely good friends and had a lot in common, or with other men— Emily had heard that a priest from Georgetown University wanted to leave the order for Jane, but that was just rumor and never substantiated. She always came home to Martin, though they did not have conversations any longer. Most nights she crept in late and slept in after the children had gone to school, and if she was gone for a few nights, one could always be sure she would come back finally.

Martin Fielding was different this time. He did not go back to sleeping on the rug after dinner, although he did work in his laboratory most weekends. But there was an edge to everything he did, as though his working parts had been set in higher gear internally expressed. Sometimes Emily was afraid of him.

Cinderella went back to cooking beans all day with

fatback and shopping on Thursdays, and Emily worked for hours in her room, stretched out on her bed sketching. Sometimes Cinderella would come up to Emily's room and sit on the bed rocking the baby. She had become quieter lately too—wiser—as if she'd seen a thing of recognizable truth and kept it to herself to fester unattended.

"Jillian's a nice baby," Cinderella said pensively one day. "Most times I'd take a plucked chicken over any baby, but I like this one. Better'n any of mine. Mine were plain bad."

"I like her too," Emily agreed. "But it's odd that Mama had her, considering."

"It's not so funny to me." Cinderella put the baby on its belly and patted her back.

"I wonder why she had any of us or even got married?"

"She likes the count of four," Cinderella said absolutely. "If something happened to one of you, she'd probably have another just to keep up count. She was raised to raise a family herself, and she's going to do that, whatever else she does."

"Or how she does it."

"Your mama's no rebel, Emily. Not like you. She just does things." Cinderella shook her head, put the baby over her shoulder and got up. "But she has a different way of doing things than most mortals. Someday . . . someday . . ." Cinderella opened the bedroom door. "You spend too much time up here in this room by yourself. You'll end up committed."

"Crazy?" Emily laughed.

"You're that already." Cinderella chuckled and shut the door.

Martin Fielding left September 1. Emily marked it down in her diary, the last mark she made for a long time. It was the beginning of her senior year in high school and Jillian was four months old.

Emily was not surprised that he left. What did surprise her was that he did not go anywhere. He simply packed his suitcase and moved into his office on Eye Street with the cancer-infested mice. He put his clothes in the closet for the patients' coats, slept on a sleeping bag on the waiting room couch and ate his meals in the cafeteria at Doctor's Hospital.

It was a time in Emily's life when she needed to know that a man, even a desperate, defeated man, could by an act of will do something about the quality of his life. It was not doing something to sleep on a yellow-plastic couch in a doctor's waiting room and eat dinner at the hospital dispensary.

Emily was disappointed in this man—who she had always believed would, if unshackled, soar like a gull.

Chapter Four

I T WAS APRIL—clear and crystal cold. Two weeks of heavy rain, beige slush pocketing the sidewalks, had dried by sunup and the air was moss-thick with spring. April nineteenth.

Everyone Emily knew had died in April. Gramme Fielding last year on Easter Sunday—two weeks to the hour after her only daughter, Jennifer, Aunt Jennifer from Kansas, who died in layers of cancer; and Tad Bricket, who rammed his motorcycle into a truck on M Street (high on cocaine, so everyone said); and just this April—April Fool's Day, to be exact—Jake Kasper (who had been trying to die since he was five years old, walking along the insides of bridges and riding hellbent down Macomb Street with his feet on the handlebars of his bike) died without any intention from a gas leak in a North Carolina boardinghouse near the university. A girl was found in bed with him. She was dead as well. Which made five people Emily knew intimately dead in April (if you could count the girl with Jake and Tad Bricket, who knew Jane O'Reilly's cousin but had never heard of Emily). And then there was Emily, who had been born in April, which must say something.

She shifted Jillian in her arm and walked up the steps to the Russells', where Jillian stayed on Thursdays, Cinderella's day off, while Jane Fielding danced at the

Arena Theatre and went shopping and to lunch and whatever else she did with her days. (Emily had seen her dance at the Arena just last week—an elegant black-and-white swan who moved mechanized without effort.)

Jillian screamed when Emily left, thrusting her small fists into the belly of Alicia Russell, who was trying to contain her; she screamed without breathing as long as she could, but Emily turned and left without remorse, walked straight up Newark Street and didn't turn back in spite of Jillian's screams sailing in front of her. She had plainly turned like her mother lately and would go to hell.

Last night there had been a fight, not like the well-mannered, self-contained arguments, free-floating like mercury balls between Jane and Martin Fielding before he went to live in his office with the mice. But a fight of consequence. Even the twins, stoic as Spartans, equal to everything, stuffed raggetys without nerves, came into Emily's room and read their library books because they were afraid to stay in their own rooms.

Martin had come to say he wanted the children. He wanted at least Emily to come with him when the divorce was final. Jane wanted the children too—certainly Emily, who would be going off to college in the fall anyway and had always lived with Jane, even during Martin's long absence in Europe. Emily could hear them even after she had gone up to the third floor, where Cinderella was ironing her hair in preparation for her day off. Whatever the outcome of the argument, it was clear to Emily that Jane would have the children.

Cinderella was bad-tempered. She wanted to read her Bible and Emily had learned to beware when

Cinderella wanted to read her Bible—the wrath of God whipped straight from the Bible, through Cinderella.

"Like as not, your mama'll win," Cinderella said, climbing into bed. "Now you go off downstairs."

"Thing is, Daddy should have us," Emily protested. "He's earned us."

"Some prize." Cinderella snorted. "It doesn't work that way. He knows it and she knows it." She pulled the covers up over her long legs, folded them just so at her waist, put on her glasses and opened the Bible on her stomach. "And I know it." She hit Emily lightly on the head with the rolled-up newspaper she saved for keeping track of the recent murders in Rock Creek Park. "Now go to bed."

Emily walked around the back of Dorsey McClarity's house and went in the side door. She would not go to school today; it was not unusual. Often lately, she didn't go to school. Dorsey McClarity left the side door of her house, which was one up from Emily's, open, so Emily could spend the day in Dorsey's room and sketch, since both of Dorsey's parents worked. All of Emily's artwork was at Dorsey's; she was there that much. Sister Marie Joseph would call at home and Cinderella would tell her that Emily had bronchitis so bad she couldn't even come to the phone, and then she'd cross herself as she'd seen Emily do in her Catholic days to expiate her sins. Once after Sister Marie Joseph had called for at least the tenth time and forced Cinderella to lie about Emily's health, when she could see Emily's blond head on the porch of the McClaritys', Cinderella marched over next door and whacked Emily with a rolled-up newspaper. After that Emily tried to skip only five days a month, but it was usually twice that.

"I am sick," she told Cinderella earnestly one night in her room. "Plain sick, as if I had a fever or a lung full of fluid."

"You got troubles," Cinderella agreed matter-of-factly. "Living in this house could make the angel Gabriel sick."

Usually Emily waited until Dorsey came home at three to find out what had happened at school, but lately Dorsey had taken up with a nondescript drummer from St. John's (whoever would have thought that Dorsey, built like a drum herself, with a round dollop of curly hair the color of orange juice on the top of her head, would ever meet anyone). Dorsey never came home after school any longer, so Emily went from the solitude of Dorsey's room during school to the solitude of her own room for the rest of the day.

The sun porch of the McClaritys' house looked over the driveway and patio of the Fielding house. Emily worked there in warm weather and she could hear the street sounds since the house was so quiet she could hear her own brain revolve. When she looked over at her own house this morning, Jane Fielding was talking on the phone. She was still in her dressing gown and it was late (late enough for St. Anne's to be calling to check on Emily's bronchitis; she should not have skipped school on Cinderella's day off). Emily watched her replace the receiver and go into the door to the library, out of Emily's view.

Then she settled down to her work. She was sketching a dancer. Lately she had been interested in dancers for the wonderful feeling of abstract movement, and she had been involved with this particular dancer for some time—she was different from anything Emily had done, concentric, flowing complete, unlike the angular, half-spoken dancers of other sketches—so at first she was too involved to hear the car pull up in their driveway. When she did look up, Martin Fielding was walking in the back door of the house. She was astonished. Her father never left the office during the day. Emily got up and leaned against the porch ledge and waited, looking, although there was nothing to see. Then, in a short time, Martin Fielding came out again, went to his car, opened the trunk and returned to the house. When he came out this time, he was carrying a large rolled rug over his shoulder. He stuffed the rug in the trunk of the car, shut the trunk, went back and locked the kitchen door. Then he backed the car out of the driveway and headed north on Lowell Street in the opposite direction from his office.

Her father had finally taken something from Jane Fielding, Emily thought to herself with a strange elation. He was not going to slink into the gray cave of an office after all but was going to decorate it with a rug from his own house and not put up with things indefinitely. It gave Emily a sense of power.

She waited on the sun porch, watching for her mother to come back through the library door to make another phone call or leave. And while she was standing there, she had an urgent need to go to school. She did not know why and did not try to rationalize it. She simply put the sketch pad underneath Dorsey's bed, went out the back door and walked up Lowell Street to the streetcar.

"I was at the doctor's about my bronchitis," she told Sister Marie Joseph. "That's why I'm late."

"That's very odd," Sister Marie Joseph replied, looming up at her like a black hawk. "When I talked to your mother this morning, she said you had gone to school." But nothing was made of it. Emily should have known something was not right to have got off so easily.

Martin Fielding picked Emily up at school that day. She stayed late for math make-up and his car was parked double on Thirtieth Street at the front door of St. Anne's. The twins sat glumly in the back seat on etiher side of Jillian, who was slumped sleeping in her car seat.

"How come you're not at work?" Emily asked.

"I thought I'd pick you up and we'd go to the Hot Shoppe."

"For a chocolate milkshake," Charles said.

"I hate chocolate," Margaret insisted. "It makes my face break out."

"Then strawberry. Do you know what, Emily?"

"What?"

"Mama's disappeared."

They drove into the Hot Shoppe, pulled up to one of the voice boxes and ordered chocolate and strawberry milkshakes.

"Mama won't let Jillian have chocolate," Margaret said. "It stains."

"What do you mean disappeared?" Emily asked.

"Just that," Martin Fielding replied without emotion. "When Margaret came home at lunchtime, your mother wasn't back from the Arena."

"So I went straight to the Barkers' and called Daddy at work," Margaret said proudly.

"You shoulda gone to the Whartons'," Charles interrupted. "They know us better."

"I called the Arena," Martin Fielding said. "She never arrived this morning. They were planning a dance for a new show and she was the choreographer," he rambled on, as he never did, bright-cheeked with an unfamiliar exhilaration. "She is very reliable about some things, you know, and this was an important rehearsal."

Emily slid down in the seat and closed her eyes. "Disappeared," she thought, alarmed. It seemed altogether impossible. Her mind, subterranean, below memory, could not settle. For months now, she had been in a dull, uninterrupted maze. The possibility of some definite chaos was not unattractive.

"Do you think she's left us?" she asked, returning her milkshake to the tray untouched.

Martin Fielding shrugged.

"Did you call anyone who knows her, like . . ." She didn't finish.

"Senator Hallow is in North Carolina for a family reunion," Martin said with a wry smile. "Mudbank, North Carolina. His secretary was very explicit." He grabbed Emily's knee playfully. "I don't think he took your mother to Mudbank with him. I don't think she'd go."

Cinderella was cleaning the kitchen like a madwoman on the evening of her day off. She even polished the porcelain knobs on the cabinets and did the icebox clear to the wilted lettuce leaves and leftover lasagne, which she usually kept for weeks. She did the floor on her hands and knees with a scrub brush, something she had never done that Emily could remember.

The police came. One patrol car with two policemen who took down information in a spiral pad; they sat in the living room side by side on the charcoal-velvet couch and spoke unconcerned in civilized tones. Emily sat in the kitchen with Cinderella and smoked a cigarette.

"You may paint black tar on your own lungs if you've a mind to, Emily Fielding, but you've no right to do the same to my country-bred lungs." She sat down at the table next to Emily, thrust cucumbers and tomatoes across the table for her to dice. "Some day off," she muttered. Emily put out her cigarette.

"Did you go to school today?" Cinderella asked. "Or don't you like Thursdays?"

"I don't like Thursdays," Emily said. She started to tell Cinderella about the rug—about standing on the McClaritys' porch and seeing her father pick up a rug and put it in the trunk—but thought better of it. She was by nature careful with information—kept it to herself until she knew what to do with it; usually kept it to herself regardless. "But I did go to school late."

"Saying you'd been to the doctor's."

"Right. How'd you guess?"

"You'll be caught someday. Lying like you do."

"It's not lying. It doesn't hurt anyone."

"But you."

"Anyway, I was caught."

"That so?" Cinderella looked up, impressed.

"And they did nothing."

She took the cucumbers and tomatoes, tossed them in the salad barehanded.

"Where d'you think she went, Cindy?"

"Your mama?" Cinderella shook her head. "Indeed I do not know."

"Off with a priest, I bet." Emily leaned forward. "Y'know, I heard from Jane O'Reilly that there's a Jesuit priest who wants to leave the order and go off with Mama."

"Emily." Cinderella looked up with level eyes and solemn. "Your mama hasn't gone off with any Jesuit priest."

But Emily wasn't convinced. She had a clear vision of Jane Fielding in her leotard with a long black shirt and black cape fleeing in a taxi, stopping at Thirty-first and R to pick up a priest, younger and more anxious than she was, who had skipped his second-period class in Chaucer, left a note on the board for his students. The cab whipped through Rock Creek Park over the bridge to the airport, and the two of them slid into the seat over the wing whispering to each other. In New York, they changed planes for Rome, and in Rome they were whisked off by an emissary of the pope's to a retreat for renegade priests and their mistresses. Emily was caught in reverie and did not hear Cinderella call dinner.

They had steak for dinner—even Jillian—and Emily sat at the table with her father after the meal and had a glass of wine. It was like a celebration.

I I

THE NEXT DAY, Sister Marie Joseph found Emily in the girls' room during athletics. She was sitting in one of the booths with her feet on the toilet seat so she would not have to play lacrosse where Michael McCarthy might see her—legs long as hockey sticks—on his way to Georgetown.

She followed Sister down the dark halls of St. Anne's close in the wake of her black robes, across the formal garden that separated the school from the convent and into Sister's private quarters, where a small gas fire was burning and tea was set for serving on a round table.

Sister Marie Joseph was direct and kind. She said that Jane Fielding was dead, that her body had been found that morning in the Potomac River near Great Falls and it was suspected she had been murdered some time the day before.

Almost immediately Emily slept, anesthetized in shock without memory. Someone, she recalled later, was at the head of the bed, someone clean-smelling who gave her an injection that made her foggy and fed her tea from a spoon, holding her head in strong arms and feeding her. When she finally woke to a reasonably clear consciousness, it was the next day. Sister Marie Joseph was sitting in an upright chair beside her; Emily asked her if she could please go home.

Cinderella picked her up in Jane Fielding's MG convertible with the top down—a turtle straining her narrow neck above the steering wheel all the way down Wisconsin Avenue. She drove in short spurts and muttered shaking her head, "Lord, Lord." She wanted

to say something to Emily, but Cinderella was no senti-
mentalist. All she did say as they pulled up the driveway of the yellow-stucco house was: "Now I know where
the dining room rug got to."

Emily went to her room, locked the door and lay face
down on the bed. Occasionally she slept, but even in
half-sleep what had happened the morning her mother
died was clear to her. Most of the time, she trained
her mind away from thinking, but once she followed
with cold precision that morning as she had seen it—
watched her father enter the house and leave with her
mother's body wound in the dining room rug; even
traced in imagination his drive to Great Falls and his
simple disposition of the black swan he had loved—and
as she thought, her mind sprung as though too tightly
wound and spun out, like electric wires gone wild, a
scene so terrible she was certain she had gone mad. But
somehow, through sleep and self-control, she remained
intact. Occasionally she thought of leaving, but generally
she was simply too tired.

She did not see Martin Fielding until late evening,
and when he did come in, sitting across from her in the
bedroom chair, she did not look at his face. Only at
his hands folded loosely across his belt. He had the
cleanest hands she had ever seen.

"I would like you to accompany your mother's body
to Philadelphia."

Emily looked puzzled.

"She'll be buried in Philadelphia."

"I see."

"Your grandparents would rather I not come, of
course."

Emily crossed her legs beneath her; her head was dizzy from having lain so long.

"Because of the separation. The Fowlers don't divorce." There was an edge of hysteria to his voice. "They stay together through everything. There have been unpleasant feelings lately. Your grandmother is quite angry."

"I'll go."

"I hate to ask you, Emily. You're young. This is not easy."

"I'm not young," she said matter-of-factly, and he did not disagree.

"Cinderella will go," he said, and then, nearly smiling, "She likes funerals."

"No," Emily said flatly, "I'd rather go alone."

"You'll go by train tomorrow morning. I've notified Lydia. Services are planned tomorrow afternoon at St. Martin's Church."

"Then I'll come back?"

"You can stay the night."

"I don't want to." She got up, sat down in front of her dressing table mirror and brushed her hair. She had not brushed her hair for two days. Her father lingered as though he had something more to say, but she did not make it easy for him—simply brushed her hair, looking at the middle of him in the mirror. When he left, she locked the door.

Lydia Fowler walked with Emily at the head of the funeral party—a tall, handsome woman, irreverently detached from the general movements of life; she could be vicious and people kept their distance.

"Forty-two is young to die," she said. "Jane would have lived a long time."

"Yes," Emily replied. It was nearly all she had said in the hours since the train had arrived at Thirtieth Street —"yes" and "no"—except to her grandfather, who had suffered a slight stroke when he learned of Jane's death and sat in his bed propped up by pillows, pale and opaque as though he were disappearing slowly and without consequence.

"Unable to cope," Lydia Fowler said brusquely of him when Emily came down from his room. "Has always been unable to cope."

In the car, after the grave-side services, Lydia asked her granddaughter whether there were any suspicions.

"Not that I've heard," Emily answered.

"I have my own," her grandmother said, looking dry-eyed out the window at the long stretches of Main Line lawns between the church and Tredifferin. "It could be accidental, of course. A robber, something like that."

"That's what the police suspect," Emily began. "And Daddy."

"But Jane could be provocative," Lydia continued, as though she had not heard her granddaughter at all. "Your father will move in with you, I presume."

"I'm sure he will."

"Who will care for the baby?"

"Daddy and Cinderella."

"You might move in with us," she offered dryly, without enthusiasm.

"I'll be needed at home," Emily said. "Besides, I'm coming to college here next year."

"Bryn Mawr?"

"No. Rosemont."

"A Catholic school." She shifted her long legs without turning her head. "I never understood why Jane raised you a Catholic."

"I had to go to Catholic school because I caused trouble in my other school."

"Certainly you could have caused trouble without being a Catholic." She got out of the car at Tredifferin. "There will be people coming to the house should you wish to spend the night, Emily."

"I'd better get back."

Their cheeks touched. Lydia Fowler closed the car door and the driver drove Emily back to Thirtieth Street Station. Cinderella met Emily as arranged in Washington; she wore a gray starched uniform and drove Jane Fielding's convertible top down in a light drizzle.

"I have bad news," Cinderella announced, whirling around the statue at Union Station. "Your father's been arrested on suspicion of murder."

"Daddy?" she protested. "He was at work."

"Mind I said 'suspicion.' " She lay on the horn. "No-count black man," she hissed at a passing car. "Suspicion means nothing."

"How come they even have suspicion?" Emily's voice broke. "They thought it was a robber yesterday. Daddy. Everyone. Even the police."

"Some lady saw your father's car or thought she saw your father's car yesterday morning in the driveway."

"But he did come. Later. He said he was there around eleven to give Mama a check."

"This lady saw him there at nine." Cinderella turned

down Lowell Street. "And Senator Hallow's aide claimed he overheard a fight between them on the elevator in the Eye Street Medical Building last week."

The street was covered with police cars. Someone took Emily's picture as she walked up the front steps.

"Leave the child alone," Cinderella spat, charging up the steps behind her.

Another man with a notebook took her arm as she went up the stairs. "Excuse me," he started. She pulled away, raced up the rest of the steps into her room and locked the door. She fell across the bed.

It was clear to her, since Martin Fielding had been arrested, she would have to make a decision about what she would say and what she would not say. She took out her sketch books, and in the dim light of late afternoon sketched dancers, dancers, dancers, bending, leaping, turning, sitting—all manner of dancers page after page. Sometime in that space of time and work, she did make a decision.

She took out her diary. The last entry was September 1—the day Martin Fielding had left home. She filled in day after day of incidentals:

I skipped school today. Wrote a love poem to Michael McCarthy. . . .

I hate drinking. After school I came up to Dorsey's porch and had a glass of wine all by myself. It made me feel terrible. Dried up . . .

I think I'll get a kitten. I'm alone up here on Dorsey's porch so much a kitten would keep me company. Only Mama's always reminded me of a cat.

She crossed out the last and decided to leave Jane Fielding out of the diary altogether.

She wrote through October, November, December, into the new year, writing in different pencils.

April 19. I was sitting on Dorsey's porch sketching dancers. I've been doing this one really good dancer—the best thing I've ever done, but I just can't get it right. Besides it's Thursday and Michael McCarthy goes down Thirtieth on his way to Georgetown at 10:30, so if I leave now and hurry, I might catch him halfway down. "H'lo sweetheart, " he'll say to me and smile that super smile. Fat chance.

Then she put the diary on top of her desk where Cinderella would surely find and read it.

Her decision to protect Martin Fielding was clearheaded and unsentimental.

II

Emily and Pia: 1957

Chapter Five

EMILY FIELDING stood naked in front of the full-length mirror. There was a small ball right between her pelvic bones, hard now beneath her palm. It didn't show front on in the long mirror. It didn't show when she turned to the side either, though at that angle, she was ample as she had never been before. Stirrings. She pressed her belly and it seemed to respond with a pulse—probably her own. The boy who had taken a shower after they made love (had in fact lain with her only a few minutes and then leapt up to bathe) came out of the bathroom and was astonished at the frankness of her naked body doubled, dimly lit in the full-length mirror. (They had made love in the dark and under the covers; even now he had on chinos but no shirt.)

She turned to face him straight on, her legs slightly apart, her body balanced at ease.

"Can you tell I'm pregnant?" she asked.

He sat down on the bed, pulled the covers up over his legs.

"No." He did not know what else to say.

"Here." She walked over to the bed where he was sitting and took his hand. He had never seen a woman naked before, except the backside of his sister—a much older sister nearly thirty—and that in the shower years ago, so it didn't count. Emily put his hand on the round hard ball between her pelvic bones.

"C'n you feel it?"

He nodded; his hand was numb. After all, he couldn't be counted on for much. He had only slept with one girl, and that three times, after he had met Emily at a party two weeks ago (where a friend—an older friend, a senior—said she was a *very* good date and winked). He was only eighteen and not much ever happened in Doylestown, where he had lived until this fall—a quiet boy, mechanically bright, president of the student government, that sort of thing, the son of a doctor, the only specialist in town, but quiet and unmistakably gentle. He couldn't be expected to have been around. All this went through his head, and he withdrew his hand, put it underneath the covers.

"It's a baby." Emily sat down beside him. "Isn't that extraordinary?"

"Yes," he replied, though nothing in the last few minutes seemed extraordinary any longer.

"Mine?" It came to him without thought or surely he would not have been so foolish.

"Thomas"—she looked at him with warm surprise— "I've only known you two weeks."

"Well . . ." He was flustered, pulled his knees up under his chin.

"This is an old baby, nearly three months." The baby pressed desire on her loins and she kissed the boy. He seemed young and unwise to her but gentle, and she liked him.

"There've been other guys?" he asked, his face ob-

vious in pain, betrayed. He had not been warned that
growing up could be so disappointing.

Emily nodded, regretting she had brought it up.
She had not told anyone else, but this boy seemed harm-
less—next to everyone else she had met—not simple-
minded but careful. She wanted someone to know about
her who would think it was important.

"Whose baby is it?"

"I don't know," she replied. "Mine."

"You don't know?" He was bewildered.

"No." She took her clothes off the chair and started to
get dressed.

"You do this?" he asked. "You sleep around?"

"This year I have." She pulled her sweater over her
head and sat down on the bottom of the bed. "Since I
came to college. Never before."

"And you have no idea whose baby this is?"

"Nope."

Her body burning with an urgent need more complex
than desire, she had made love to anyone without self-
recrimination, without interest. Their names swung
through her brain like old memories that no longer
mattered. Only this boy who had touched her with his
honest innocence, perhaps—at least with his lack of the
conventional cruelty she had come to know as the constant trade of boys in college. It was January, and
Martin Fielding's trial for murder would begin in May.
In May she would flunk out of Rosemont College. The
nuns had told her that it was inevitable unless she got
to work on subjects other than art, but she did not get
to work and spent the hours she was not in the studio
lying on her dormitory bed, a book for a pillow, her

hands pressed between her hot knees. She had a reputation after the first week away from home. She would do anything, so everyone who knew about her said, but she took the responsibility for it without regret.

"My father's a doctor," Thomas said suddenly. "Surely he knows someone. You know—someone to sort of do a secret job. It happens all the time—like there was this girl in my high school, a really nice girl," he insisted.

"Nope," Emily said flatly.

"No?" he swung his legs off the bed, pulled on his shirt. "How come?"

"I don't want one."

"Afraid?" He was struck with the possibilities for heroism in the moment. "Maybe you could stay here with me. I don't care what you've done. You know, something might even come of it."

Emily pulled her hair back in a barrette.

"Emily?"

"I don't want to stay here," she said, and turned on the overhead light so the dismal room of the Fortieth Street flat was flooded with light, articulating its barrenness.

"I've got to get back to school," she said. "It's nearly twelve."

He grappled through his closet and came out with his coat.

"No," she insisted. "I'll walk to the station myself."

"It's a terrible neighborhood. A girl was raped on Locust the week I came here. Right on the street." But already he'd put his coat down.

"I'll be okay," she said. "Bye, Thomas."

"What are you going to do about the baby?" He tried to detain her.

"Have it."

"Keep it?"

"I want a baby." She walked out the door onto Fortieth Street.

Somehow he knew he would not see her again, at least not in the same circumstances—or anyone like her. Exhausted, he crawled into bed in his pants and shirt and fell asleep with the light on.

Fortieth and Locust was dimly lit. She turned up Locust towards the train. Ten blocks. The streets were dead empty and she could hear the echo of her loafers on the pavement.

She had not intended to get pregnant, but she had not done anything to avoid it either—or for that matter even thought about it, as most of the girls in the dormitory seemed to do, innocently, as though one copulated by inclination—so there must have been intention in spite of her reasonable mind.

She had arrived at Rosemont the first Tuesday in September and hated it as she had expected she would. Her room was already done up with pennants from Villanova and Pennsylvania and Yale and St. Joseph's High School. There was a full-length color photograph of Eddie Fisher, fleshy and bright purple; the desk was covered with gilt-framed pictures of boys, identical long-toothed, large-mouthed versions of a younger Eddie Fisher, signed "To Shari, all my love forever," and a whole cheerleading uniform, red and white, was pinned to the wall over the other bed. The roommate, Shari,

put in a request for a room change once a week like
clockwork from the first day Emily arrived. Sister Eva
told her "Forbearance is a virtue" and "Do unto
others." It was Shari who first noticed Emily was pregnant and told everyone she knew in whispers not to tell
a soul.

The first night at Rosemont, Emily met a boy from
Villanova, a senior, prowling, kept just at bay, come
to look over the new freshman class, lingering in the
lobby. Emily must have told him what she wanted without knowing—some kind of chemical communication
(which she found out later and used with intention), but
for the moment, she was amazed that the boy from
Villanova took her for a long walk and then to his
car, where he made love to her, burning hollows in her
unexplored body, neatly so, without the incompetence
of Tommy Stealer. Afterwards, she lay exhausted, at
physical peace for the first time in months and searched
with vague interest the boy from Villanova's face, but
it was a face smudged, imperfect, undistinguished, like
all the faces bearing down on hers in the weeks to come
as she became an easy prey for any stalk—not prey
either, for it was with full consciousness that she sought
these moments for quick release, a stay against her own
impotence, her unmanageable brain surging volcanic,
unreleased within her skull.

They were all ordinary boys. Mostly Catholic, mas-
ters of quick sex to an end without meaning—boys of
simple intolerance, with Irish faces and bellies soon to
liquefy in flesh. Blameless but cruel. She would never
care for any of them and that was how she wanted it.
There were many, many. Only one (not counting
Thomas) who had lasted more than two weeks, and

sometimes, often, she was out every night in a week in the back of some ill-fitting car, on the couch of a cheap Main Line apartment. She did not want to make love to someone who could matter. It was for the process simply. After months of dark wakeful nights, she slept black sleeps without dreams, and when she woke in the morning with the memory of her mother, a blue bathrobe belt tied tight as a package around her neck (for that was how she had died, Cinderella finally told her), she knew that in several hours she could lie on the floor of some old Pontiac and lose consciousness.

In December she found out she was pregnant. She was not surprised. What did surprise her was her great happiness as she walked from her first visit to the doctor on Thirty-fourth Street. She was going to have a baby. It gave a magnificent sense of clarity and purpose to her life.

Emily reached the second-story platform for local trains just as the last train pulled out for the Main Line. She watched the red light beat staccato against the darkness and the last cars thrash between the cement banks.

"Missed it," the man at the gate said.

"Yes."

"Better take a taxi," and he clattered down the steps in front of her. "Oughtn't stay around here, pretty girl like you."

Emily reached into her wallet and found, as she had remembered, a dime and a return ticket to Rosemont. So she couldn't take a taxi.

She followed the redcap down the long steps through a hollow tunnel that connected the local trains to the major station. The terminal was nearly empty. The candy and newspaper stands were closed, the drugstore was closed, a boy came in, deposited a stack of newspapers next to a concession stand and left, a cabdriver drove up, parked, looked around and left. There was no one in the information stand.

There were two men—young men in jeans and leather jackets, long hair greased to stick straight out above the nape of the neck like chicken feathers, rough-spackled skin, hard as asphalt. They sat a distance from each other, arms stretched against the wooden seats, unrelated but obviously together. One smoked. He smoked with his first two fingers, tilted his head back and blew the smoke in a long, thin stream above his head. When he had finished the cigarette, he snapped it behind him. It was still lit and Emily could see the pinhead red glow on the tile floor. The other man ate a candy bar.

Emily sat down on the bench across from them. Initially she crossed her legs, then arranged and unarranged herself, unaccountably self-conscious. The man eating a candy bar wadded up the paper in a hard paper ball and threw it at her. It hit her in the shoulder. When she looked over, he was grinning at her straight on and, from her distance, it looked as if he had lost his front teeth or else they were black with chocolate from the candy bar. Emily did not smile back. The young man nodded to his friend and they both laughed, hollow in the empty station, like laughter in a trash can.

At the far end of the bench, the same bench where the men were sitting and across from Emily, a man sat reading a newspaper. He was an immensely fat man, well dressed. When the young men laughed, he looked from behind his newspaper momentarily.

Emily rested her head against the bench, mildly oblivious to the fact that she had an hour to get back to Rosemont before the large black wrought-iron gates swung closed and she was campused for the month. An intensity of the moment blocked her brain. She felt as if there were a high drama acted out before her of which she was inadvertently—or perhaps not so inadvertently —a part. As if these two young, unattractive men, heads cocked like roosters, observing the terminal as though it were in fact teeming with people, had something in store, and she by some quirk of circumstances or design was victim or instigator. The vacuum air in the tobacco-smelling space was electric with expectation and she did not know whether it was her expectation or theirs. She did know her hands were wet with fear—wet as spring streams, and she wiped them on her winter coat, rubbing them vigorously against the knubby wool texture one at a time. As she did, the young man with the candy wrapper got up, stood spread-legged like a greased fowl and wiped his palms on his jeans, first one then the other—mocking. He did not need to laugh but he did— loud and long—a strange jungle squawk, and Emily started. Their eyes met and she had to smile. The situation demanded a response, but the smile, such that it was, simply replied to cold terror. He started to walk towards her, summoned. Had she summoned him? Were there forces within her acting beyond her control? He ambled, rolling on his hips, throwing his legs out before him, dead certain like an animal of his possibilities. The other one, his long-lipped twin with the cigarette between the first two fingers, got up too, stretched above his jacket so his blue T-shirt came out above a bare flat belly black with curls.

There had been a smash-up when she was very young. Perhaps seven. A splash of glass littering Emily's cheeks sharp and cold as spring water—a sudden swirl with an accompanying sense of doom like the final lurch on the roller coaster, and the car stopped, smelling of rubber. The man in the other car, a small car without a top, leapt over the side and threw up his arms, shouting at Jane Fielding in a foreign tongue. Jane let her head fall back against the seat.

"Damn," she muttered. There was a nasty cut over her left eye.

"You ran a red light, lady," he barked into the car at her in English. He was small like his car, dark and rumpled as an avocado, with his sharp black eyes that snapped into the car at both of them, took in everything at an instant—the child Emily, the impeccable Jane Fielding with a bright red gash above her eye, the fine upholstered English car, out of place in wartime.

"And nearly killed me," he sputtered. "And that child of yours. A rich, careless lady who drives cars with velvet seats. Ach!" He threw up his hands and spat. "Blood," he said ominously.

Jane sat up, looked out on the road.

"Blood?"

He spat again. "Blood."

She opened the door and got out, remarkably calm.

"And you have ruined my car," he shouted, but his voice had lost its anger. "Of course," he muttered, "you have ruined my car."

Jane adjusted her skirt, walked over to his car, running her hands over the dented front door, bending down to look underneath the wheels as though she were intimate with the workings of machines. She leaned against his car then, half-sitting on the front bumper, her skirt pulled halfway up her calf; the avocado man stood next to her, no longer shouting now, talking with his hands and smiling occasionally, a large toothy smile that wrinkled his face in the sun. Emily could not hear them from where she sat, still in the front seat, but she could tell just by the manner of the man that he was no longer concerned, and while they stood there together, there was an exchange, some unnecessary shift in Jane Fielding's body, which spoke sufficiently to Emily's memory that now, years later, she knew she had seen a hateful thing of which she was also capable. When they walked back to the car, he was solicitous. He helped Jane Fielding into the driver's seat, held her arm in an olive grip, and Jane smiled at him. A rare, open smile. There, for the first time in Emily's experience, she knew the frank power of sex—the female animal, giving off scent, subduing to entrap.

"Don't worry." The man smiled. "I will say nothing to the police." He took the bill she gave him and put it in his pocket. "I will call you at the number, right? Six, five, eight, three. I'll remember."

"Fine." Jane started the engine, put the car in gear and drove off waving gaily.

"Whose number is that?" Emily had asked.

"Stupid man," was all Jane Fielding answered. "Simple-minded. Easily won."

"Alone?" The young man sat down beside her, not too close. Emily did not answer. "Pretty easy to tell you're alone," he said. The pulse in Emily's ear roared above the sound of his voice. The other young man walked over to a vending machine. Emily did not watch

him, but in the empty terminal, she could hear him
deposit a coin, pull the silver lever. She heard the thud
of candy or cigarettes and then the easy walk across the
tile floor to where she was sitting. It was clear to her—
in that moment immaculate; these two young men were
going to have her and something in her sex had allowed
it—perhaps invited it. Whatever, there it was and she
was her own victim, like Jane Fielding with a bathrobe
sash tied around her neck.

"Madeline." It happened so quickly, Emily was not
even aware until the warm, genial face of the fat man
behind the newspaper was upon her, bending towards
her bright as an apple.

"Madeline, dear child. How splendid to see you.
Imagine." She started to protest, but he was in absolute
control. "Here I am waiting for the last train to Washington in the middle of the night, mind, and there you
sit silent as a mushroom, not even acknowledging your
old Uncle John—though surely there's none so fat as
me around. Even in *this* city, where there's absolutely
nothing to do but eat and drink." He was crazy, surely.
Emily pulled back from his face close upon her but did
not look away. "How is your mother? Surely the last
time I had dinner with her I thought she'd aged ter-
ribly, was nearly senile, in fact, and not yet fifty. But
you look not a moment over twelve."

The young men had slid away. In the corner of her
eye, she saw them first under the freedom statue and,
though she could not see them any longer, she heard the
heavy glass doors open and suck shut, so she assumed,
relieved, they were gone. The fat man heard them too,

sat down a distance from Emily and cleared his throat.

"I'm not Madeline," she said coolly.

"I would be astonished if you were," he replied.

"You would? I thought you knew me."

"I have never in my life seen you."

Emily frowned. "What were you doing, then?"

"You were about to get into trouble. Did you know that?" He took out a cigar, tilted it in his mouth and lit it with great ceremony. "I save these as rewards for myself for moments of heroism," he clucked. "Do you mind?"

"No." Emily looked at him curiously. "You could tell something was going to happen?"

"The air stank of it."

"I thought so too," she said.

He chewed ceremoniously on the end of his cigar. "What are you doing here in the middle of the night, anyway?"

"I missed my train back to college."

"And will be late and in trouble."

"Right."

He shook his head. "I suppose you haven't the money to take a taxi."

She nodded.

"Young people today are so hopelessly muddleheaded. They never carry money, as though they thoroughly expect it to bloom full grown at their feet." He reached into his pocket and pulled out a bill. "Now let's go find a taxi."

He walked with effort, considerable huffing and puffing, although he was not old—simply too large to be supported by two legs.

"This is very kind of you."

"You find me on a good day," he said. "Some days I am villainous."

A taxi was outside the station, the driver sleeping in the seat, his feet out the window. The fat man pressed the money in her hand.

"Do not take such risks again, Madeline," he admonished. "You are too young."

Emily settled in the back seat. When she turned to thank him, he already was through the glass doors and padding down the corridor.

"To Rosemont College," she told the driver. When he drove through the black gates just as they were being closed for the night, she was asleep.

Martin Fielding was in splendid spirits. He arrived at Rosemont at eight the next morning to meet his weary daughter for breakfast.

"I called you last night"—he locked arms with her—"and you were out. You look beat."

"I am." She lengthened her step to keep up with her father's long stride.

"I was up for a medical meeting at Penn yesterday and thought I'd spend the night just to have a chance to see you and you're out," he teased.

"Sorry," Emily replied.

"Sister tells me you're always out."

"And in trouble with my studies. Did Sister tell you that?"

"That too." He gave a brisk jump, leapt around facing her and swung her in his arms. She had never seen her father frivolous.

"Daddy." She grimaced.

"She said you are too good an artist not to be in art school."

"Which means I'm too bad a student to be at Rosemont."

"She was very complimentary." He laced his arm through hers and kissed her cheek.

"You look awful, Emily. Don't you ever go to bed?"

"Some."

"Is it that you've fallen in love?" he asked.

She shrugged.

"I fell in love twice," he said. "The first time with a girl who married an ex-football player on our spring vacation without a word to me about it." He swung her hand in his. "My luck has not been good."

"Mine either."

"So you haven't fallen in love."

"No."

"Don't." They walked up Lancaster Pike into a doughnut shop.

"I won't," Emily said in earnest. "I really won't."

"Good for you. It's hardly worth the confusion."

It was a serious conversation shot lightly back and forth to camouflage. They both knew it.

Emily had meant it. She had been astonished at the control she had of inclinations; she had become a hard-bitten, unromantic woman, invulnerable.

The real matter at hand was Martin Fielding's trial for the murder of his wife.

"Cinderella says you keep a diary," he said over coffee.

"Has Cindy read it?"

"Of course."

Emily laughed. "I did," she said. "I haven't since Mother died."

"Well, there is a problem come up and I'm hoping perhaps you can help me with it." He drummed her fingers lightly with his own. "The prosecutor apparently has a witness—a surprise witness—we don't know who, but she, I imagine it's a she, thinks she saw me around the house at nine on the morning Jane died."

"But if you weren't there?"

"These things happen, Emily. You have to have an airtight defense. I wasn't there, but someone thinks she saw me and is willing to go to the stand on it." He shifted in his seat, talking quietly without intensity, as though it were an incidental conversation. "Cindy did read your diary. Nothing is sacred with Cinderella, you know. And when I told her about this new witness, she told me about your diary. She says there is an entry the day your mother died saying you were on the Mc-Claritys' porch painting until ten o'clock."

"I guess I remember that." With effort, she kept her eyes on her father's.

"If you were on the porch until ten o'clock, surely you would have heard my car if I had come to the house."

"I guess I would have."

"Then would you go to the stand in my defense?"

"Of course." Emily broke.

"Don't, Em," he said, uncomfortable. "I'm sure it will be fine without you—it's just that having you will be an assurance."

He thought she cried because she believed he was innocent, and walked back to the college with his arm around her shoulder, moved by her belief in him: She thought it extraordinary, beyond her understanding of things that they could love each other as they did and boldly lie.

Back in her dormitory room, Shari Sargent slept on her back, her chin tilted towards the ceiling, and snored like an old dog. Emily lay down, closed her eyes and shut out the room with all its pennants and boyfriends, bland-faced musical heroes, incidentals of the transitory life around her. Someone in the next room or down the hall played Elvis Presley. Beneath her palm on her belly, a pulse beat with new life.

Chapter Six

THE TRIAL of Martin Fielding began the eighteenth of May, a year after Jane Fielding's death. He had been arrested shortly after her death and released on bond pending this trial, which was expected to be short —possibly less than a week. Emily came home from college three days early. The fact was that she had left Rosemont College for good, but she gave only Cinderella that information because she was the only one to whom it seemed to matter. Martin Fielding wandered absently around the house in the days before the trial, slapping an old newspaper against his flat palm, leaving cigarettes burning on the edges of tables and with his fly unzipped—this fastidious man of great reserve. Jillian had taken to eating poisons from the bottom kitchen cabinet—dishwasher liquid, Ajax, simple poisons, mainly—and climbing up on precariously high places, often falling. She had a knot the size of a golf ball on her forehead, and more than once Cinderella had sped to Children's Hospital in Jane Fielding's convertible with a screaming Jillian in the back seat off to have her stomach pumped or her brain scanned.

"I wasn't meant to have children," Cinderella railed. "The Lord knows I don't even like them."

The twins, self-reliant, contained, spent the weekend

before their father's trial reading and playing board games. When friends called, they said they were spending the weekend with their father, apparently resigned that it would be his last weekend with them. An atmosphere of quiet doom pervaded the house.

"I don't understand," Emily said, sitting at the kitchen table with Jillian on her lap. "It seems like everyone just expects him to lose."

Cinderella dashed around the kitchen, dressed in churchgoing clothes and a new hat, a brown mixing bowl with a bunch of artificial cherries, blood-red, hanging on the side. It made her look like a plastic tree.

"Really, Cinderella," Emily had exclaimed when she saw it.

"A lady has to have a hat for things like this," Cinderella snapped back. "And look presentable." She squashed the hat square on her head. "We have an impression to make."

"I thought he had a chance," Emily persisted.

"A chance," Cinderella said with authority. "But from the talk I've heard around here, it's not going to be as easy as how do you do." She mixed up a bowl of soup for Jillian and set it before Emily so that she could feed her. "Now when my cousin, Anderson Stokes, went to trial for shooting his wife—which he most certainly did do and she hasn't a bit of feeling in her right arm to this day—we all knew he was going to get the book thrown at him, and we just went along to court as a neighborly thing to do."

Cinderella was by way of an expert on crimes. She pored over newspaper accounts, followed murders to their conclusion, cataloguing the sequence of events if not in fact at least in her mind, and tried to attend the trial of every relative or friend no matter how remote; there were a surprising lot of them. It was in all counts hard to believe that she was not looking forward to Martin Fielding's trial. She had arranged to take the twins to school early all week so she could be at court by nine (had told Martin Fielding she must drive Emily, who oughtn't be driving alone in her condition, but Martin Fielding was only vaguely aware that Emily was pregnant). She had found her sister's daughter-in-law's cousin to take care of Jillian; she had cooked and frozen dinners for the whole week, including desserts, and she'd bought two new dresses—one red, to go with the cherries on the hat that she was wearing at the moment and the other beige to go with the hat. It was certain that she planned to be equal to this occasion. She even had the corns on her feet fixed after twenty-five years, she confessed to Emily, not that anyone would notice.

"And the truth is," she said, going on nonstop at a pace, "Anderson got off scot-free, so you just never know. Prepare for the worst"—she lifted Jillian in her arms and marched up the back stairs—"and you're never disappointed."

It wasn't until all the children were in bed and Martin Fielding off to his office on the Sunday night before the trial that Cinderella finally mentioned Emily's baby.

Emily was sitting in the kitchen drawing and Cinderella came down in her robe, her hair done up in rags, sat down at the kitchen table across from Emily and drank a bourbon straight—something she simply never did except in the privacy of her own room.

"Still making pictures?"

"I'm going to art school," Emily said. "Well, not art school, exactly. I'm going to be an apprentice to a sculptor in Philadelphia."

"You're not going back to college." Cinderella took an apple from the refrigerator, shined it on her robe and set it down in front of Emily. "You better eat for two."

"I have to leave college."

"Flunk out."

"Nope, for a change." She finished the leg of a dancer, held it out, shook her head and started again. "Matter of fact, ever since January I've done well. I'm leaving because the Sisters aren't keen about unwed mothers." She took a bite of the apple. "It might give some of our girls ideas, Mother Superior said."

"Oh, yes, indeed," Cinderella said. "I'm quite sure those ideas never crossed any of their Catholic minds." Cinderella leaned forward on the table and looked up at Emily. "Who is the father?"

"I don't know."

"You don't know," she said.

"That's right."

"Emily Fielding." Cinderella gave a low laugh. "Quite a little time you've had away from home, child."

Emily raised her eyebrows.

"Like your mama, huh?"

"Cindy," Emily said, astonished.

"Well?"

"No, I'm not like my mama. You know that. I'm not like her a bit."

"I hadn't thought so."

"I'm decent to people."

Cinderella grabbed her arm, but Emily pulled away.

"Shut up."

"I'm sorry, Emily."

She folded her arms tight across her chest.

"I was wrong, simply wrong. You're not like her, child." She rubbed her tired eyes and took another swallow of bourbon, from the bottle this time, straight. "But what in God's name is a nineteen-year-old child gonna do with a baby?"

"I'm going to keep it."

"All by yourself?"

"Of course."

"You're more foolish than I ever thought, Emily."

"It's not foolish," Emily said quietly. "Keeping this child is the only simple decision I have ever had to make."

Cinderella shook her head, brushed Emily's long hair out of her face.

"You obviously don't understand," Emily protested. "I had thought you would."

"I understand," Cinderella said, wrapping her long arms around Emily's shoulders, pressing the blond head next to her broad chest. "It's just that you're the fairest-haired black woman I ever knew."

I I

THE FIRST TWO DAYS of Martin Fielding's trial were uneventful. The prosecuting attorney was a bright Harvard boy who had prepared his case thoroughly, relentlessly, because it would matter in his real future after this two-year tour of duty in the district Attorney's office; but he was overzealous, appeared in fact very silly next to the defense, Archibald Clover, an older man of gentle Southernness who belonged with Martin to the Chevy Chase Club, that bastion of civilization that had for generations survived political Washington untainted, with its gentlemen's tennis and afternoon teas. It was certainly clear to Archibald Clover that a man from Chevy Chase would not kill his wife, and he prepared his defense with just that sense of quiet outrage. Martin Fielding, for his part, appeared unlikely as a man of passion—self-effacing, courteous, soft-spoken. The judge was almost apologetic to have brought him there.

The many who had come—patients of Dr. Fielding's; curiosity seekers who had read about it, since it was front page on the Washington *Post* with the international news; Tommy Stealer, who sat right across from Emily and stared unembarrassed at her belly, as if there were a flamingo perched there; even Sister Marie Joseph, who most certainly believed that she did God's will to come and show the Fielding family her support (fortunately able to rationalize in this way any pure instinct such as curiosity)—they were all powerfully disappointed. Nothing happened in the first two days of the trial that was not already old news.

There were several pictures of Jane Fielding taken after she was found in the Potomac which Emily was encouraged to look at. She was able to assume a new distance, a part of the protective skin she had lately grown, thicker and harder at the tears. The picture of her mother was unfamiliar, unrelated—even when Cinderella, who looked carefully at each print, her long neck craning beneath her cherry hat, gave low grunts of disapproval in her throat like a pigeon. Emily had learned from the unrelieved chaos of her life, that order, her personal sense of order and surely her survival, depended upon the distance she maintained from human contact—she must learn to live self-sufficient, uncommitted and inviolate. She arranged relationships, amoeba-like, with a technician's skill at self-protection —and thus she was able to dismiss her mother's lifeless body and make incidental love with the same detachment. She was not invulnerable but careful and, given the immense purpose of her unborn child, intact.

The second day of the trial began with certain anticipation. The *Post* that morning had carried the defeated Senator Hallow's statement about his relationship with Jane Fielding in which he contradicted himself, saying first that they were good friends and then that Jane was a tease who had countless relationships. He concluded his statement by saying that his own personal relationships had never been better, which was obviously discountable since Mrs. Hallow still lived in the house in Spring Valley and the senator lived in the Westchester; they were never seen together. (Besides, Mrs. Hallow had written Martin Fielding on the Saturday before the trial, wishing him deserved good fortune and saying that it had all been a terrible business, obviously meaning to include herself.)

"Lotta hogwash," Cinderella said, putting on bright purple lipstick in the courtroom Ladies'. "That senator couldn't tell the truth if he saw it printed on a Teleprompter."

"Blot your lips, Cindy," Emily said, conscious of another lady in one of the compartments listening to them. "The purple clashes with the cherries on your hat."

"Mind your own lips, child," Cinderella snapped.

By the end of the second day, however, there was a feeling in the air that something was about to happen.

"That green snake has something up his sleeve," Cinderella announced to Emily on the way home, referring to the bright prosecuting attorney. And Emily acknowledged that Cinderella was probably right.

The twins and Emily were sitting at dinner that night when Margaret said to Emily, full of rancor, "I suppose you don't know what Mrs. Boynton said."

"No. I suppose I don't unless you tell me."

"Well, Andy Boynton told me"—she wiped her ten-year-old lips daintily with a napkin as if she were approaching seventy—"and Andy absolutely always tells the truth. He has a reputation for it."

"How boring."

Margaret shrugged. She was a very quiet child who seldom spoke at home except to Charles, but when she did speak, it was frequently to destroy.

"Mrs. Boynton says it's horrid you're going to Daddy's trial pregnant without a husband," she said; "that you'll prejudice the jury against him."

"Mrs. Boynton can go to hell." Emily got up and pushed her plate away. "And so can you." She clattered up the back stairs to her room.

Margaret and Charles exchanged glances.

"Now see what you've done," Cinderella said. "You kept her from eating her pie and her as thin as she is." Cinderella licked the lemon from her long black fingers.

"Thin." Margaret squealed.

"Thin." Cinderella smacked her hand hard. "You're a hateful child, Margaret Fielding," she said, finishing Emily's pie herself. "Plain hateful."

Emily went to bed with the door locked, but she did not fall asleep until just before dawn, and then she slept fitfully.

I I I

ON WEDNESDAY, the third day of the trial, Estella Knowland was brought to the stand. The coup witness, the surprise, dragged triumphantly from the aging house in Cleveland Park where she had been born sixty-one virgin years before. Miss Estella Knowland. Spinster, malevolent churchgoer. She had the kind of justified power to destroy that comes of aligning one's soul with doctrinaire goodness. She had come to do her Christian Duty.

She walked to the witness stand in an orderly blue suit and a box hat like Cinderella's without the cherries. She carried a lace handkerchief in her small freckled hand and spoke distinctly with vicious assurance.

"I don't care for children a bit," Estella Knowland had told Martin Fielding without apology years before, when the Fieldings first moved in next door. "They wreck my rose garden and trample all over my ivy."

"I'll make sure mine don't come on your property, Miss Knowland," Martin had said.

"I'll see to that," Miss Knowland had replied, but she did not have to worry. Her house loomed, haunted as a ghost house, over the Fielding children, and not a one of them ever dared let a foot pass over the imaginary line of property.

"Bloody bitch." Jane Fielding had said that night when Martin had reported on Miss Estella Knowland. It was one of the few times Emily could remember her parents in accord.

"Miss Estella Knowland," the prosecuting attorney began, "where were you on the morning of April nineteenth, 1956 between the hours of nine and ten?"

"I was where I always am. Back by my kitchen window doing the breakfast dishes."

"Can you see the Fielding house from your kitchen window?"

"Plain as day. My kitchen window looks right over the Fielding driveway and into the bay which is their dining room." She was enjoying herself, standing straight and proud, round and healthy as a plum. "We use the room with the bay as a parlor," she added, as though it might be a convincing detail.

"What did you see the morning of April nineteenth while you were doing the dishes?"

"I saw Mr. Fielding drive up in his car. A red car with the top down. You couldn't miss him if you were blind. He drove up the driveway right under my window and I said to myself, 'How odd him being here so early in the morning,' since all of us knew they were separated. Mr. Aiken down the street had first told me about it a few days before."

The judge intervened to inform her she must answer only the questions asked.

"You saw Mr. Fielding go in the house?" the prosecuting attorney continued.

"The back door. He always went in the back door. Why, I've known what they were doing in that house for years."

"Was Mrs. Fielding there?"

"Her car was in the garage and I had seen her sitting in the dining room in her gown drinking her coffee just a few minutes before Mr. Fielding came. I remember I thought to myself at the time, 'What a shame a lady like that being left with four children to raise.' "

The judge intervened again.

"How long would you say Mr. Fielding was in the house, Miss Knowland?"

"Fifteen minutes." She looked at the jury for approval, and then said decisively, "Yes, it was fifteen minutes."

"And all the time you were doing the dishes?"

"I'm a thorough housekeeper," Miss Estella Knowland chided.

"I asked, were you doing the dishes?"

"The dishes. Yes, I said I was doing the dishes," Miss Knowland replied, annoyed. "I did the last dish at nine-thirty exactly."

"Did you see Mr. Fielding leave?"

"I did."

"Was there anything unusual in the way he left?"

"There was," she said triumphantly. "He left out the back door carrying a rug over his shoulder. I watched him open the trunk of the car and put the rug in. And I thought to myself—"

The judge spoke before she could continue, the courtroom had shifted and buzzed.

"The next day, Mrs. Jane Fielding was found dead, in the Potomac River; nearby was a rug from the dining room of the Fielding home," the prosecuting attorney sang. "Why didn't you say something at the time, Miss Knowland?"

Emily did not hear Miss Estella Knowland's answer. A flood of nausea overtook her. She struggled across Cinderella and her family, ran down the side aisle of the courtroom and vomited in the corridor just short of the Ladies'.

A kindly policeman helped her to a room where she sat thick and wet, shivering, when her father came in alone, shutting the door behind him. He sat down across from her.

"Whew," he said. "Bad luck. Archibald suspected this."

"Everyone knows Estella Knowland goes out to do the marketing at nine just after we leave for school," Emily blurted. "She is a very predictable lady."

"Even in the worst weather, she's out by nine," her father agreed.

"So she could not have seen you."

"She could have seen me come had I come before nine, but she could not have seen me leave."

"And, anyway, we *know* it's not true."

"Of course it's not true," Martin Fielding said quietly.

"She's been put up to it," Cinderella said, marching into the room unannounced and shutting the door firmly behind her.

"Put up to what?"

"Put up to believing she saw Dr. Fielding walk out of the house with a rug over his shoulder when she was halfway to Connecticut Avenue by nine-fifteen and couldn't have seen the house if it was blazing to heaven." She smoothed her dress, straightened her hat and sat down. "Someone has made Miss Estella Knowland see things she plainly could not see from the canned-goods aisle at Safeway." She crossed her arms victoriously. "Or paid her to see them."

Martin Fielding shook his head. "I can't understand it," he said.

"My cousin Anderson Stokes offered me one hundred dollars to lie on the witness stand," Cinderella said. "But, I'd have no part of it."

Emily took the witness stand for the defense at four. She was sick and weary with the strain but controlled, as certain of herself as she had ever been. She had a larger responsibility than she had anticipated. Since morning, since Estella Knowland, there had been a different feeling in the courtroom, a new interest in Martin Fielding.

Cinderella stretched her neck so as not to miss a thing. She was proud of Emily, proud of the way she stood straight and brave with child, proud of the way her hair fell accidentally around her simple, open face, proud of the strength in her voice, which carried conviction in its tenor. Cinderella squared her hat on her head, folded her long fingers in her lap and listened to Emily's testimony with the approval of the successful mother that she believed she had been to this white woman's child.

"Emily Fielding, you are the eldest child of the defendant?"

"Yes."

"You were of course aware that your parents did not get along?"

"Yes."

"Where were you on the morning of April nineteenth?"

"On Dorsey McClarity's back porch."

"Which is next door to your house?"

"Yes, it overlooks our backyard."

"You were supposed to be in school?"

"Yes."

"You commonly skipped school?"

"I skipped school on the morning of April nineteenth," Emily said. "Yes, I commonly skipped school that year."

"What did you tell the teachers?"

"I told them I was ill."

"What were you doing on Dorsey McClarity's back porch on April nineteenth?"

"I was drawing."

"How long were you there?"

"Until ten in the morning. From eight-thirty, when I took my sister to the baby-sitter's, until ten."

"Have you any possible proof?"

"I have the proof that I arrived at ten-thirty, in the middle of math class."

"We know that your father was in his office at ten-thirty on April nineteenth because he saw a patient, and that he came over to deliver a check to your mother after lunch on the nineteenth and found her gone. If he also came to the house at nine that morning, could you have heard his car from the McClaritys' porch where you were drawing?"

"Yes, I could have."

"And you didn't."

"No, I didn't."

The following cross-examination by the prosecuting attorney was swift and pointed.

"I would like to suggest to you, Miss Fielding, that you were indeed sitting on the back porch at the Mc-Claritys' between nine and nine-thirty—that you heard your father's car drive up in the driveway, that you saw him leave with the dining room rug, put it in the trunk and drive off. Then you went to school because you knew something was wrong."

"No. That is not true," Emily replied. She was in control. She had been warned. Her stomach churned, but outwardly she was self-possessed.

"Have you any proof of your activity that day?"

"I have the diary which you have seen." She pointed to the diary on the table in front of the courtroom with other tangible evidence, including the blue bathrobe cord that had been around her mother's neck. "I wrote in the diary before I went to school."

"Who is to say that you did not write in the diary later—two days later, after you were convinced of your father's guilt."

"I am," she said. "I am testifying under oath."

"And we are asked to believe the oath of a child who skipped school and lied that she was sick, who was expelled from another school and failed most of her courses, who had a reputation and now stands before us obviously with child and without a husband," he said evenly. "We are asked to accept the word of a woman like that. Your Honor—"

The judge intervened. "You are absolutely out of order."

"You are a child of mine," Cinderella said when Emily sat back down, and she gripped her hand. "A child of mine."

On Friday, the fifth day of the trial, Martin Fielding was acquitted on the basis of insubstantial evidence. Estella Knowland broke down under cross-examination and gave conflicting reports of her activities on April nineteenth. That was Thursday. On Friday the jury recessed for two hours and came back with the decision. The court was dismissed by noon.

Cinderella went home, took off her beige hat with the cherries and her new dress and sent home the daughter-in-law's cousin who had been sitting with Jillian. Martin Fielding and Emily joined Archibald Clover at the Chevy Chase Club for a drink, and Emily took the late-afternoon train back to Philadelphia. At the station, Martin asked her when she would be back and if she would be all right living alone in West Philadelphia; he did not once mention the baby she would bring with her the next time she returned to Washington. On the train, Emily took from her purse the envelope her father had given her as she embarked. In it was a substantial check and a note scrawled in her father's awkward hand:

"Emily—I am grateful to you for your loyalty this week. I try not to think how much trouble these years have probably been for you. My love, Daddy." For a moment, she wondered what he meant, or if he meant anything at all. She suspected, as was surely true, that it was simply an expression of the urgent need of a lonely man to touch the life of someone who mattered to him.

I V

IT WAS A BRILLIANT June morning bold with late spring butterflies and trees in full green. Up from sleep. There were other women chattering around her, above the insistent television, fat-breasted women, very young, eating breakfast from aluminum trays. Emily pulled herself up on the starched pillow and looked at them.

"Have a baby last night, hon?" one woman asked her, bright blond hair in plastic curlers, made up before breakfast. Emily nodded. The other two women perked up.

"Terrible, wasn't it?" one woman said. "I threw up right there on the table."

"Did they do you like they do the rest of us?"

"I don't know." Emily looked confused.

"Well, you haven't got a husband, have you?"

She shook her head.

"This is the ward for the girls without husbands," they cackled.

"Didn't they make you go through the whole thing wide awake till you thought your ass'd rip off right there on the table and then, when it was all over worth putting out for, they slap gas over your face so you're out cold and wake up vomiting?" The woman in curlers finished off her breakfast with relish.

"I was awake," Emily said. "I didn't want the gas."

"No kidding," the first woman said.

"Women with husbands get shots in their back so they don't feel a thing." The woman in curlers got out of bed and slapped into the bathroom in paper slippers.

"So you saw your kid, huh?"

"Kind of," Emily said. The doctor had not told her that there was a special room for her because she didn't have a husband.

"We've never seen our kids," a tiny girl child in the bed next to Emily said. "We're not supposed to go to the nursery."

"They can't keep us away," the girl said from the bathroom, where she'd left the door wide open so as not to miss a thing.

"I don't want to," the girl child said.

"Why?" Emily asked.

"Because it's being adopted. I mean, none of us will keep the kid. They're all being adopted." The girl looked at Emily curiously. "Isn't yours?"

A nurse appeared in the door before Emily had a chance to answer. She was holding a small, tightly wrapped bundle.

"Emily Fielding?"

"Yes." Emily sat up. The nurse looked around the room at the rest of the women, then back at Emily, her brow furrowed.

"Emily Fielding?" she asked again.

"I am Emily Fielding."

The nurse picked up Emily's arm, checked the hospital identification around her wrist and then checked the number on the tiny wrist inside the blanket she was holding.

"I guess you're it." She shrugged. "How come you're in this room?" But she didn't wait for an answer. "This is your daughter. You want us to call anyone for you?"

"No, thank you," Emily said. "You could pull the curtain, though."

The nurse pulled the four sides of beige cotton curtains, leaving Emily in a small, dim room the size of her bed.

When the nurse had gone, Emily unwrapped the baby, took off her diaper, her tiny undershirt, and inspected her back and front, her fingers with nails the size of pinheads, the crown of Oriental black hair, the miniature toes that stretched and separated. There was a small brown strawberry mark in the middle of her stomach; otherwise she was perfect.

III

The Afternoon Following the
Funeral of Martin Fielding:
July 19, 1966

Chapter Seven

DEAR CHARLES, Margaret and Jillian,
Daddy was buried this afternoon—a steaming, cloudless Tuesday afternoon with a steady heat coming up from the ground where we left him. The flowers, tilted like toy carousels against each other, had wilted before the crowd dispersed and I wanted to take off my shoes, grind my toes in the short stiff grass and run. Although my kinship to him has been the largest I have known—except to Pia, and that, of course, is different—I am relieved he is dead. Sitting here in his study, the room where our mother fiercely bedded a score of ordinary men while we slept innocently enough on the story beneath her, the same study where our father must have spent many dreadful and lonely hours —sitting here with the rest of you properly greeting the curious mourners in the rooms below, I feel an unfamiliar calm and know it grows steady in me because he is dead.

Lordy! Mrs. Hiram Pinckney's here—"Muffy"— when she blew in the front door in her purple suit looking like a hothouse iris, I knew I had to get out of there or explode. Sometimes this week, I have thought that Daddy died in self-defense—his only out, for she

would have caught him sure. He was never much good
with women, you know. Thoroughly a doctor, I guess—
quite proficient in parts but not much with the whole.
Muffy was around at the trial—pale pink it was then
and huge hats. She was subtle enough that I did not
notice she was there so much, but once he was acquitted,
she moved in with blazing feathers and possessed him—
pale specter in a white suit. He went back to his research on mice just to stay in nights. Poor Daddy. I hope
he will be allocated a purgatorial division reserved for
Men Only—at least until the judgment.

You've done nobly, the three of you—altogether sane
and collected as I watched you standing in the living
room this afternoon greeting people, some of whom,
many of whom, have not been inside this house since
Mother's murder (were probably checking the floor for
bloodstains beneath their dainty black veils. Ah, to have
come so close to civil war and yet remain intact!). Standing with you, the first-born, the oldest child, I felt
estranged and out of sorts, as if we had come from different seeds, perhaps, and mine, congenitally deformed,
grown lamely to a defiant womanhood, did not fit with
the rest of you. So I came up here—through my old
room, which I left at seventeen, now done over in fluff
for Jillian, smelling sweet and dusty of cologne. When
I lived there, I had mud-brown spreads on the bed
which wouldn't show the dirt, Mother said, and James
Dean hung on my inside closet door. I kissed him passionately before I went to bed at night, until at last
his paper lips disintegrated and his kisses had the taste
of paint.

I never came into this study when I lived here. It
was out of bounds because of Mother, and by the time

Mother died, we had come so accustomed to not coming here that Daddy was never disturbed. It is a pleasant room. You can see the tops of the trees out of the dormer windows and the Cathedral towers seem to be floating free-form. I expect you can see to the Potomac in winter when the trees are bare.

I am losing myself in this room with the smell of our father still about the desk, as though he had just stepped out for a moment and will be back shortly to infuse the space. I came up with the purpose of writing you a letter to tell you something about all of us, to explain in part perhaps, now that Daddy is no longer accountable, that strange sister who went off and had a baby out of wedlock and lives, so you all believe, without proper regard for form.

The first time I saw our father was in the spring of 1945 and I was seven. We had left Tredifferin, where we had lived throughout the war, and taken an apartment in the Westchester to be ready for him, come back a daughter's hero, an old man worn thin at thirty-five whose medicine could not be used on blasted Jews. We did not come to Washington alone. A man named Anthony Call came with us, stayed with us up through the last night before Daddy's plane arrived. He would sit in a fat stuffed chair in the living room, call me an "odd pussy without a tail." They would laugh and Mother would rub his knee with her bare toes. The Westchester was a pleasant-enough place to be; Mamie Eisenhower lived there and other war widows, but I particularly remember Mamie Eisenhower; I used to wonder if she had guessed about Anthony Call.

I was beside myself the day that Daddy came. He had written me letters through the war; I had pictures of him, not many, and those I did have were filched from Mother's album, but I had studied every part of him in the secrecy of my own room. (I never—have never—shared a thing that mattered to me with Mother. My deepest recollections of her were of a fearsome woman capable of some destruction, and though as a young child I often crawled into her lap and sought a kind of refuge in the slender, sweet-smelling curve of her arm, we had nothing between us.) I had looked for my nose in his nose, the cast of his eye in my own, and found nothing but a vague familiarity in the whole of him, since I resemble only Lydia Biddle (some demonic plan of the gods to remind me at every reflection of my own baseness, I suppose, since she is nasty to the core. I suspect she has the power to turn men into frogs). It is Jillian who looks like Daddy, right to the fat big toes.

He was a very quiet man, Martin Fielding. That is the first memory I have of him after he got off the plane in Washington. I later found him to be a gentle man of dignity but dangerous reserve who seemed certain and self-possessed, which he was not. And I loved him deeply, though in the last ten years it has been at a distance, as you will understand.

Mother was a striking beauty with a kind of chemistry that I used to think was simply evil but I understand now as that paradoxical combination of sensuality and cold indifference that many people cannot ignore. I used to be quite proud to be around her, particularly at school, and though I never had a lover before college, boys I knew from other girls who dated them would stop by to see me just to have a glance at her, and she'd oblige in a slim black dressing gown.

I don't believe I ever loved her, or if I did, my love

was so inextricably bound by fear of her that it was never sustaining. I wanted her to think well of me, but by the time I was twelve, I suppose I had concluded that she thought nothing of me at all—neither well nor not well—so I distanced myself from her such that when she did die, I was primarily shocked by the way in which she had died, amazed that there could be an end to her but not moved by her absence. Although certainly her death has changed the way I have lived in a way that her life never could have.

I sound very cool about her, which is nonsense. I can afford to be cool now she's been dead all these years. But I wasn't a bit cool then. She scared the hell out of me. I never defied her, never betrayed her, never thought an ugly thought about her without such an immense sense of guilt, certain that she knew, wherever she was, every thought I entertained.

And what a life she led! Forty lives in forty years without regret. She was never satisfied. She would try on a new life as though it were a dress, pose at different angles in the three-way mirror, at first elated by what she saw and then with indifference or disgust, she would unzip it and toss it on a chair. I saw her do this many times.

She was a powerful woman and had a hold on me I can neither understand nor totally get rid of. It had something to do with her great beauty—a godless, primitive beauty that takes into account only graven images and said to me as I was growing up—wanting, surely, for that is basic and was unsatisfied by the pale Catholicism offered in the place of parental love—Jane Fielding said to me wordlessly in everything she was:

"I dare you to believe." And I never did, never have. That is some hold on a growing child.

I'm sure that Cinderella has told you that they fought and separated and that is probably all Cinderella has ever told you—that and her own secure wisdom on marriage: "A man and a woman don't belong together anyway, what with the way things always get to between them." I can hear her now.

To say they fought is only partially true, because they only fought the last few days before Mother's death and then it was over the custody of us and not about each other at all. What they did was to destroy each other— Mother, bit by bit, killing Daddy like cancer does, slowly, teasing with hypocritical weeks of remission followed by months of multiplication and unbearable pain. And Daddy killing Mother in fact.

Once, when I was still quite young, Mother hit a small gray cat. She always drove low, sleek cars and drove them very fast. This morning on the way to school, she was as usual driving very fast; a cat ran across the street in front of us, thudded like a drum against the tires, first front then back and flipped as if jet-propelled into the curb by the side of the road. She did not stop. I did not ask her to or expect that she would; but even now I can see the lump of gray fur boomerang, then throttle out its life and stiffen. I mention this because the last definitive fight between our parents started with a cat.

I was sitting in the living room reading after supper. No doubt you were all in bed, though I was never consciously concerned about you. Mother swirled in the door like a hurricane, straight from a dance practice, a long cape swung over her spare leotard—and shortly afterwards, Daddy came, still in his white coat. He rang the bell first and then walked in. Mother had thrown her coat on the back of the couch and was standing in the hall reading the mail.

"I thought you were coming over tomorrow night, Martin," she said, flipping the mail back on the table. "I have to leave again shortly."

"My office is open tomorrow night."

"It seems as if you're always on call." She slid into a chair by the fireplace. "You've hardly time to take off your coat."

"Jane," he said. "You hit one of the Marleys' cats just now."

She flung her face against the chair-back in mock melodrama.

"I was behind you." He sat down next to me. "And you just hit the animal and went on."

"Animals cause more accidents than drink, Martin."

"You could have stopped, at least."

"I will tell Anna Marley tomorrow." She raised her eyebrows. "Honestly, Martin, you've grown soft as jelly ever since you took up with your mice."

"I just stopped by the Marleys' a few minutes ago and told them."

"That was good of you. You apologized for me, I expect." And then she mimicked him, "My estranged wife, Jane . . ."

"You're a careless woman."

He had come to see Mother about me. I knew all about it. He wanted me to come to live with him as part of the divorce settlement, and they talked about it with me in the room for a short time—Mother edgy because she had a performance that night, Daddy with contained irrationality. In the end, getting nowhere, he said, "Why can't we leave it up to Emily? She is eighteen."

"Leave it up to Emily, then."

"Emily?"

I did not answer.

"You ought to understand, she will not leave here, Martin," Mother said. "She'll visit, I'm sure, but this is her home."

"I don't believe you."

Mother shrugged. "She's afraid to leave."

"Afraid of you," Daddy shouted.

"Of course, of me." She left then and Daddy stood next to the couch, raging silently.

"I suppose she's right," he said to me.

"She is," I replied honestly.

I had never seen his anger so absolute.

Two days later, I stood on the porch of Dorsey McClarity's house and watched Daddy stuff the dining room rug in the back of his car. Instinctively, subconsciously, I must have known what had happened, because in the hours that followed, I never told anyone that I had seen him. The following morning, Mother's body was found on the banks of the Potomac near Great Falls. The dining room rug was found nearby.

I have kept my counsel and lied at his trial without regret.

I know it is too simple to say that in the absence of God, Daddy needed a sustaining, personal love, a commitment of energy, and it was bad judgment on his part that he married Mother. She lived without consequence. It must have been innate, a genetic trait, like the color of eyes, as though the soul, for what it's worth, is chemical, at least in fact. There was no comprehension of commitment at all. She ought never to have married or mothered or been a part of any lasting arrangement, for she wanted to live, was constructed to live, day to day without regret or condition. Daddy was a possessive man—a fact I can neither explain nor illustrate with him but simply know in a way I know myself to be so. It is perhaps a need that we all have for a union of spirit, which becomes in me, as it must have with him, too often confused with a desire to consume another human soul—I am certain that this in Daddy irritated Mother, and irritated, she was cruel. She was self-possessed in the clearest sense of the word.

The rest of the story you know as well as I do—better, since all of you remained behind to live with Martin Fielding.

I had intended to close with a justification for the way I live. Reading the letter now, I think it is unnecessary. It is certain that I am afraid to marry. I know enough of the personal destruction rent by that association in my genes to be fairly certain there has got to be some deformity of my soul.

As for Pia, to bear her and raise her alone was an instinctive decision. I am as certain of its rightness as I was at one time certain of the mercy of God. I have wanted above all things in living to be a good mother— and I have been.

Love,
Emily

She folded the letter and put it in her wallet; sometime, perhaps next week or later in the year, she would mail it. Not yet.

IV

Emily and Stephen: 1966

Chapter Eight

THE AFTERNOON SUN slid hot silver through the angles of long, thin buildings, dividing and distorting the figures beyond the glass front of Gallery Fontani and Fifty-second. Through the window, Emily Fielding shimmered in angled triplicate like one of her own paintings.

It was Emily's first New York showing and the gallery was crowded—full to bursting of starched cotton dresses in pastels, wretched with the thick, sweet smell of Woolworth's perfume, spun cotton hair against the bold, pure color of Emily's primitives, the stark whitewashed walls. The champagne was gone by two; the ladies on the bus from Jersey slipped rose-petal tea sandwiches into their handbags for the trip home. Not the usual gallery crowd surely, for this group, most of it, had come to see Laura Rand—not the paintings of Emily Fielding at all. From Jersey they'd come on the Greyhound and from Upstate New York on the morning train into Grand Central and even from as far off as Philadelphia, where Emily lived when she wasn't in New York filming "Better Promises."

She stood now with a child's awkward grace in the second archway and greeted the people who had come to see her—not the art dealers or the critics or the spindle-legged models in spider-web jerseys who filled an empty afternoon at these showings with high conversation and champagne punch. These did not want to meet her at all—but the plain ladies who stopped the ironing or came straight home from work not to miss a single episode of "Better Promises." These canceled Saturday shopping and the appointment at the hairdresser's and the church bazaar to come to the city and meet the real Laura Rand. (The *New York Times Magazine* had an article on Emily's show, and for a week before the August 28 opening, the network had mentioned Emily right after the second commercial just in the middle of the daily episode of "Better Promises.")

"I could've told you about that Trevor," one lady from the Greyhound told Emily. "He was no good from the start. You fall for the worst of them every time."

"I wrote you a letter about it," another lady behind her piped. "You like to broke my heart when you let that man push you around. Innocent. That's the trouble with you, Laura. Plain innocent."

Emily laughed. "Someone else writes the script," she said. "I have to fall in love with whom they tell me to."

"It's a shame they work it that way," the first lady said. "I'd have a mind to tell them who I did and who I did not want to fall for."

Then a small woman, serious, bespectacled in a sea-green shirtwaist from the fifties, moaned, "You're so tall—and freckled. And I thought you had darker hair." She shook her head. "You just don't look like the same person at all."

"Better Promises" was in its eighth consecutive year. Laura Rand, like Emily, nearly thirty now—still vulnerable, untouched, with a kind of invincible child's innocence that some on the show (like Trevor Morris and Andy Brown, residents of Hughesville who had devastated Laura one episode or another. She never learned!) were urged to shatter; most others, like the ladies from Jersey, remembered an innocence in themselves and wanted to protect it in Laura.

At nineteen, Emily had gone to New York to another showing with the sculptor to whom she was an apprentice, and was sitting in a restaurant (Pia a baby strapped on her back and sleeping) when the producer of "Better Promises," Al Caparni, had seen her—sat watching her for an hour, so he later said. As she got up to leave, he had slid into the booth with her, had told her he was looking for a Laura to play a role in his new soap opera. She had to be clumsy and shy. "Innocent," he'd said, and Emily was perfect.

"Innocent?" she had laughed afterwards walking down Forty-Second Street with the sculptor.

"You are innocent, Emily, in the real sense," he had said. "It's just that you don't behave in an innocent way."

So she had auditioned for Laura, had been chosen straightaway (she was, in fact, a good if untrained actress), and for nearly nine years now had gone regularly to New York, first to film live episodes, and lately, several times a month, to tape shows in advance. Due to Laura, she was comfortable, nearly rich, in fact, for a woman alone with a child to raise. Laura was one of the major subplot characters on "Better Promises" and Emily was making nearly thirty thousand a year by the sixties. It gave her the rest of the time to work in her studio, on her sculpture primarily, although it was her paintings that sold. That were selling today, as she greeted the four o'clock ladies.

"Emily," Cloman, who had planned this show to the last detail, was tedious and intense about it, urged her, "there are people here you *ought* to see."

A broad lady in a J. C. Penney's ensemble with a bowler hat pressed through, but Cloman had Emily firmly in his grip, moved her away from the archway where she had been standing for two hours.

"I think you've seen enough of these other people," he said. "I've seen enough of these other people."

But just as they turned into the back room, where the art dealers were and the critics, the room where all of her best and latest sculpture was (they'd stayed up half the night arranging it), just then, she saw Stephen Williamson walk in.

"Are you coming?" Cloman brushed her hair out of her eyes. "Honestly, Emily, you look like something the cat dragged in."

"I guess." She scanned the crowd at the entrance for Stephen. "What did you say?"

"You haven't heard a thing I've said. Not all afternoon. Damn it, why don't you just decide you're going to be a television queen and stop painting. You drive me crazy."

"Mmm." She pulled away, wound her way through the crowd, loose-limbed, flushed with color. "Excuse me," she said over her shoulder to Cloman, "a friend I haven't seen for a long time just came in." She went through the second archway looking for Stephen Williamson. Fact is, she had only seen him once before.

In late July. She had gone to Stephen Williamson's house in downtown Philadelphia at Thirteenth and

Delancey for a party, invited there by another psychologist colleague of his from the Institute, who never had arrived that afternoon at all.

Emily did not mind. She had sat in a fat leather chair and read from a large text on family therapy (which was dull and made her sleepy) while the rest of the party got quite seriously drunk on vodka with something. Once she fell asleep and Stephen, who had come to change the records next to her, squeezed her knee. She had opened her eyes, smiled and stretched.

"Laura Rand." He sat down on the rug beside her chair. He was a large Irishman, her height but substantial, with a thick gray beard and merry eyes, deeply wrinkled in the corners, intensely blue. "I think you are not so pure as Laura Rand, Miss Fielding."

"Perhaps," Emily had said, "but Laura's thoughts are not so pure."

"Probably not," he had agreed. "You do have a reputation for being unconventional."

Emily shrugged. "What is that?"

"I suppose it's because you've never married. You haven't, right?"

She shook her head.

"Every woman I have met in America wants to marry. For no reason at all. Just to be married."

"I have never been in love."

"You don't want to be?"

"I guess not," she had said. "A person has controls that way, don't you think? That's your job, to know these things, isn't it?"

"One of the reasons I got into this job," he had said, "was to learn about controls."

"I hate psychologists, you know," she said, leaning back in the chair. "They're so nosey."

"I suppose it's safer to hate us than not."

Later in the afternoon she got a call from Pia saying that Charles had called from Washington and her father was ill. She asked Stephen if he could take her home, which he did, waiting in the car for her while she packed a bag, took Pia to a neighbor's. He was going to drop her at Thirtieth Street Station, but instead he drove her all the way to Washington. She protested only once, and on the ride down was mostly silent.

She did say, "I expect he is already dead," and put her hand down next to his expecting him to take it; he didn't.

"Are your parents dead?" she had asked.

"No," he replied, "they're still living."

"In Ireland?"

"In Belfast," he said. "My wife is dead."

"I'm sorry," she had said, and didn't ask him about it. But she did sense a kinship with this Irishman whom she knew about already, although she'd just met him. West Philadelphia was a small city unto itself and often people who did not know each other knew about each other. She knew he was a psychologist, was known particularly for his work with children and women, that he had been something else in Ireland, a minister, perhaps. She also had heard that something bad had happened in Ireland to make him come to America in the first place.

It was a strange trip through a hot, foggy dusk of Sunday afternoon—southbound traffic down I-95 beating a high pulse around them; kicking up a dust that whipped imperceptible filaments of late dry summer in their faces, in their eyes. A strange communion which bred a necessary silence, precious and careful, as though I-95 could go on indefinitely, was welcome to go on indefinitely, through the Baltimore tunnel and under the rest of the earth, to preserve this moment.

When they had arrived at her father's house, the yellow-stucco house just inside Washington, he had kissed her and he'd never called her again.

She had thought about him since. Once she had walked with Pia from Forty-fourth and Pine to his apartment at Thirteenth and Delancey—thirty blocks. It was dark when they got there and no one was home. Twice she had called him and hung up when he answered the phone. She hadn't done that kind of thing since she was sixteen.

Occasionally in those two months, working in her studio to get ready for her first show, Emily would feel an odd and unfamiliar gaiety as though she could fly out the studio roof and sail over the trees, upside down brilliant orange with her heels in the air, a helium balloon. It was an unaccountable lightness.

"It's funny, Mama," Pia said once, making a B-2 satellite on the floor of the studio while Emily worked. "You've been so queer since Granddaddy died."

"Queer?"

"Y'know." Pia shrugged. "Happy."

"Mmm." Emily considered. She had been happy.

"Like me," Pia said. "Younger than you are."

On the train coming home from Martin Fielding's funeral, Emily had gotten light-headed on one glass of wine. Sitting in the club car by herself, she was suddenly disassociated from the ground, without serious considerations or limitations or controls at all. It had something to do with the death of Martin Fielding, as though his absence on earth released her from the responsibility of who she had been, gave her the freedom to live unfettered with no claims on her from the past. Life-in-death not bittersweet with memory but entirely fresh and vulnerable.

Something else had happened too, which had to do with Stephen Williamson. Emily had lived a calm and sensible life since Pia's birth, rigid with disciplines, unencumbered by involvement except with Pia. There had been men moving in and out of her house with the haste and insignificance of jack rabbits—one for six months, none for more than that. As Pia got older, perhaps five or six, she asked whether one or another would be her father, but soon learned from her mother that these men were incidental acquaintances, occasionally pleasant, even funny or gay, but never important.

"Will we ever get a father?" she had asked.

"No, Pia," Emily had replied, "I doubt you will. I'm not the sort for marriage. Perhaps you will be."

But something was different since Martin Fielding had died. First off, she had had no lovers.

"Nobody's been here for so long, Mama," Pia said one night as they were packing up Emily's paintings for New York. "Don't you have any friends now?"

"Guess not, Pia." She had laughed. "It's nice, just the two of us sometimes."

"It's okay." She helped her mother carry a bust down the front steps. "I suppose it's always been just the two of us anyway."

Emily thought about what Pia had said, though. She had been hard at work this last month since her father's death, unconscious of the way she was living, day trips to New York to film an episode in the life of Laura Rand, late evenings after Pia was asleep in her studio— and that strange, magical lightness all the time as though she were disembodied.

I I

STEPHEN WILLIAMSON HAD AWAKENED before dawn the morning of Emily's exhibition with a sense of emptiness akin to loss. It was not unfamiliar in the years since he had left Ireland, and he had learned what to do when the day began vacuously—how to fill it with details, insignificant of themselves but mounting in number to a kind of fulfillment not altogether satisfactory.

The woman in the bed next to him snored unoffensively on her back; he slid out of the covers, not to disturb her, went into the study to make notes for Monday, notes for Mrs. Anne B. and Arthur B., whose marriage of eighteen years had never been consummated, notes for the talk he would deliver to the seminarians at Philadelphia Theological Seminary on the "Right to Love," neatly ordered in columns under Monday, and when the bright morning sun cleared his second-story window, he had written nothing at all for the seminarians or Mrs. Anne B. A kind of desperation aggravated the usual order of his brain.

The bright yellow card on his desk read:

EMILY FIELDING
Gallery Fontani, 136 East 52nd Street
August 28–September 13
Opening Tea, August 28 2–5

He dressed in jeans and left the apartment, walked down Delancey to Ninth Street where Chez Moi sold croissants hot for ten cents and Georges gave him coffee with real cream free in exchange for advice on Maria's hot flashes and general bad temper.

'So what do you think you do with that Laura Rand?" Georges asked this morning.

"Emily Fielding." Stephen told Georges things he told no one else. He trusted him. Georges was working class and so was Stephen—educated working class, but he understood his roots. "I'll do nothing with her."

"You need a woman. You are too lonely, Stephen," Georges said to him over the morning paper, "and she is very pretty."

"I like many women." Stephen laughed and spread his arms to make a yard. "None too close."

"You lie to me," Georges said. "And you a man of God."

The day was bright, clear, and Delancey Street was empty as Stephen walked back to his apartment with a small sack of croissants for the woman in his bed.

He had met Emily Fielding one time last month, but he had known about her for many months, maybe years. He knew she lived near him in West Philadelphia with a child who had no father (*no idea* who her father might have been, so the word was) and that she, so everyone said, slept around.

"With anyone, as far as I can see," his good friend, Dr. Amos Little, who was a psychiatrist at Penn, had told him, coming to Stephen for advice several months before. "I could have had something with her—something good, and I would have liked to play it straight, have dinners, go home at night to my own bed and send her yellow roses. But Emily wants nothing like that," he insisted, "just a good lay."

"Now, Amos. You're a better psychiatrist than that," Stephen had replied. "Everyone is looking for something more than a good lay."

Stephen had watched her on television. One of his patients had said once after a particularly unsuccessful session, "You want to know who I am, Dr. Williamson, you watch "Better Promises." I'm Laura," she said, her fingers wrapped around each other. "Laura to the bone."

He found Laura an uncommon television actress, as she was meant to be, tall, awkward, but lovely as a loose-limbed unkempt English child is lovely—fresh and finely made, but she was no help to him with his patient.

So he did know Emily Fielding before he met her at a Sunday-afternoon party at his apartment and was curious about her in spite of himself. He had driven her to Washington when her father became ill that day, overcome by a need to be with her, to have her closed in a car with him for several hours, and when they had arrived at her family's house just inside Washington, he had kissed her; the pounding in his groin spread through his body, was more urgent and complex than simple desire. He did not understand the nature of romantic love. He did know it unsettled the state of things and that it had to do with an abiding curiosity about another human life. He had only been in love with Margaret, and that slowly, growing since they were children on the West End from point to point like a broad bush doubling in branches with the season until she died the week before her twenty-ninth birthday. That was ten years ago and he would be forty in the fall. He did not want to fall in love again.

He did not call Emily when he got back to Philadelphia, although he watched "Better Promises" if he didn't have a four o'clock appointment and he thought about her. He found his mind slipped away from him when he was writing or working alone and she was there. It was disquieting. For years now, the emotional texture of his life had been his work. And that was fine.

Margaret Wiliamson had died in February, 1956, going into a vegetable market in Belfast. A bomb, tossed by a member of the IRA, had exploded and she had died four days later without regaining consciousness. It was an accident. The baby she had been carrying for seven months was removed by Caesarean section on the day of the accident in the hopes it might be saved, but it was already dead. Stephen was the pastor of St. Matthew's Easton Square at that time, a working-class Methodist parish, his Protestant grandmother's district in the West End, where he had been since he left seminary. But he could not remain after Margaret died. He did not have the stomach for God any longer, and it made no sense to deal with the spirit of people when his own spirit was gone. So when he had an opportunity to study psychology at the University of Chicago, he left Ireland for good. It was not a curious move; if he could not cope with the workings of the heart, then surely he ought to be able to satisfy his need to understand whatever it was about the nature of man which compelled him by studying the workings of the mind. It was safe and distant that way. Uncommitted. He had confined relationships with other people to his patients, who went home to their own homes to live their own lives.

And now Emily.

"Adela." He spoke to the woman, just waking in his bed. She was a woman like many of the women he had had since Margaret died, willing to put up with an uncommitted relationship or afraid of anything else. "I bought croissants." He took his clothes from the closet and went into the bathroom to change to dress clothes.

She was sitting up in bed when he came out.

"I'm going to New York."

"New York?" she asked.

"To an art showing of a friend."

"I thought we were going to see a movie."

"Maybe next weekend."

"Oh." She slid back under the covers. "Okay." She didn't seem to mind, or if she did, she was not going to let him know it.

Standing on the platform at Thirtieth Street, the Saturday ten o'clock Boston train roaring black soot into the city, Stephen was himself again. The long emptiness sped out of him, streaming behind in Philadelphia and North Philadelphia and South Jersey, and he felt himself in tune with the locomotive rushing to New York.

I I I

STEPHEN GLANCED through the main room of the Gallery Fontani. Emily's paintings, which stood in bold squares above the afternoon dresses and pale seersucker suits of the crowd, were simple primitive oils, but her sculpture, the enormous child giants, mildly distorted forms of men or women lunging out of stone, caught unfinished in rough rock, were plain disturbing. He stopped at the first one inside the door—a simple classic face in repose, abundant hair of a woman, hands broad and muscular of a man, and legs, half legs, struggling in rock, as though in running to be free they'd sunk, solidified without form. *Springtime, 1964,* it was called.

A group of seminary students from Philadelphia were there, very drunk even at a distance, standing under a jungle cat in black and yellow. He recognized them as some of his students.

"The good Dr. Williamson." A lanky young man in jeans and an Indian shirt embraced Stephen. "Come lend us your Irish tenor."

"I've already lent you my Irish whiskey."

"Not enough of it, Father. We're absolutely dry."

"Come off with us tonight, Stephen. Get a woman and we'll have a good time."

"I'm too old," Stephen said.

"For women?"

"For your good time."

"You've still life in you, Dr. Williamson," the first seminarian said.

"You're not forty yet."

"A week to go."

"Good God," the first one said, "I don't believe I've ever talked to a man as old as you."

"Take Emily then, Dr. Williamson. We hear she's good for aging men. Right, Stanley?"

"Has plenty of energy," Stanley agreed.

"Shut up." Stephen reddened, moved on before he betrayed himself, cut loose the trembling fist in the soft belly of the man next to him. He was a quiet, self-contained man of gentle spirit and graceful humor, but angry he was fearful. Everyone sensed that in him and was cautious. The seminarians laughed without gaiety and moved on.

Stephen went through the first room into the next, less crowded, with hard, flat benches, and sat down. Next to him was a laconic form in stone reminiscent of prehistoric man.

Emily Fielding was at the far end of the white-washed room, dwarfed by the vast bulk of a nude woman in textured canvas behind her. She was talking, her body young and generous in movement; the long dress, too large, hung on her like a grain sack, emphasizing the sharp angles of her shoulders, giving her long slender body a childlike lack of grace. Seeing her now, his mind's memory of her, held these last weeks in tight reserve, cascaded, filled the even rhythm of his body with excitement.

Behind Stephen, in fact behind the prehistoric man in stone, using the square, useless buttocks for a book-rest, Pia Fielding squatted, deep in *Dr. Strange, Master of Mystic Arts*. When Stephen leaned back against the wall, he saw her and knew at once she was Emily's daughter, something in the body of the child, in spite of her black hair and olive skin, the broad, high cheek-bones of an Indian girl.

"H'lo," he said.

"H'lo," she answered, snapped shut the comic.

"I'm Stephen Williamson," he said. "You must be Emily's daughter."

"Yes," she said. "Pia."

"You look like Pia," he said, getting down on the floor with her, sitting cross-legged beside her. "It's good your mother named you that."

"She says so, too." She stuffed her comic into her backpack. "I'm not supposed to read comics," she explained. "Only *Wind in the Willows* and stuff." She offered him a very flat tea sandwich from her backpack. "Thing is, I'm not good at school."

"No, thank you." He turned down the tea sandwich. "I was no good at school either," he said sympathetically, "always failing Latin."

"Mama failed everything," Pia said solemnly. "Even responsibility and cooperation. That sort of stuff. I do okay in that."

"Dreadful," Stephen said. "But your mother seems to survive quite well for failing responsibility and co-operation."

"I guess," Pia said hesitantly. "I think it's because she's a little famous. I didn't know that till I came here today."

"She is famous. I dare say half the people in the United States know your mother."

"Do you?"

"I do. However, not very well," he added. "I met her

once the day your grandfather was ill. You called my house to tell her."

"He died," Pia said matter-of-factly.

"I'm sorry."

"It's okay. He had a heart attack. Mama says it's best he died quickly."

"I suppose that's true." Stephen took out a small cigar. "Do you mind if I smoke?" he asked. "Whenever I am having a good time, I like to smoke."

Pia shook her head.

"It seems we always have to make a deal with death by saying that the way in which it comes is best." He stood, took off his tie and jacket and sat back down with Pia on the floor. "Tell me, is your mother like Laura Rand?"

"Laura Rand is kind of boring, a goody-goody."

"You don't watch her?"

"Sometimes. Mama never does," she said. "She's better than Laura Rand. Sometimes she does bad things; she says it's in her nature."

"What kinds of bad things?"

"Ordinary kinds," Pia went on anxiously—glad for someone to talk to, to try to interest after a morning alone. "Last summer we climbed the fence into the Germantown pool and hid in the bushes when someone called the police, and"—she crossed her legs, lowered her voice, enjoying her drama—"she danced on the table at El Toreo's. We went with Mike and I came because we couldn't get a baby-sitter. Mama danced on the table and Mike was so furious he left without us."

"Good riddance."

"Do you like my mother's work?"

"I particularly like her sculpture."

"That's what she wants to be. A sculptor. Not Laura Rand at all. Only it's her paintings which sell." She spread out her skirt. "Do you think I look bad in dresses?" she persisted, anxious for this new friend to remain and talk to her.

Stephen considered, "No, I think you look quite good in that dress."

"I hate dresses." She fussed with her skirt, tucked her legs under it. "Do you have any daughters?"

"I have no children at all."

"Oh."

"But," he added, sensing a moment with this child that touched a wire in him long insulated. It had something to do with Emily Fielding, a reawakened sense of possibilities, but also to do with the child herself. "I had a child."

"Is she dead?"

"It was stillborn."

"Was it a girl?"

"I don't know. I never asked the doctor what it was. At the time, I didn't want to know. Sometimes now I wonder, was it a daughter?"

"I guess it probably was a daughter," Pia said. "I haven't got a father." She shrugged. "He didn't die or anything. I just don't have one."

Emily had found Stephen. She moved across the room, slowly, interminably, her long dress spilling off her shoulder, her hair piled up, falling in sheaves, balanced precariously as an urn on top of her head. She had long arms and her walk was at once strong and hesitant, like the walk of a long-distance runner.

"Hello," she said, her smile awkward, fresh. They shook hands, Stephen scrambling up from the floor.

"Hello." He helped Pia up. "You remember me?"

"I do."

"You do?" He was surprised and laughed, unassuming. "Well," he said, spreading his arms to indicate the room, "thank you for asking me to come. I think you must be good, but it's hard to see for all the people."

"It is crowded," she agreed. "Most of them, I don't know."

"I think a group has come to see the work of Laura Rand."

"They must have." She laughed. "One poor lady came all the way from Connecticut; she says she watches the program every day, and when she saw me, she nearly cried. Said I was too bony, that I looked plucked as a chicken and wouldn't do at all." She wrapped her long arms around Pia's shoulders. "You've met Pia."

"Pia and I have known each other for many years."

They sat down on the plank bench. "You've come to meet someone in New York?" she asked.

"Well, yes." He had not planned what to say to her. "I am meeting someone for dinner. Later. In fact, quite late," he added, "but I felt out of sorts this morning so I just decided to come early and see your show."

"That was kind of you," Emily said. "It's over at five."

"Then maybe we can have a drink," Stephen suggested. "I'll take Pia with me now and be back to get you at five."

"Okay." She got up. "I'm staying here the night, as the gallery's open all day tomorrow." Then she laughed,

girlish, open. "Well, I'm not sure what that meant. I'll
see you later."

She watched Stephen and Pia walk out of the gallery;
on the street, he took her hand high in the air, swung
her around and around and then raced by the glass
front, out of sight.

I V

"MAMA." Pia grabbed Emily's arm. "You bumped into
that lady."

Emily stopped dancing, breathless, broke from
Stephen. "Where?"

"That one. There in the blue dress."

Emily ran over. "I'm so sorry," she said. "We were
dancing, you see."

"Yes," the woman said, straightening her dress. "I
could see that."

Emily fell against Stephen.

"We are very sorry, madam," Stephen said, but she
turned and left.

"It must be late," Emily said.

"Eleven," Pia replied. "And we haven't eaten dinner."
Stephen handed her the tea sandwiches from his pocket.

"Stephen." Emily linked her arm through his. "You
were meeting someone for dinner."

"Hopelessly stupid of me," he said. "I seem to have
missed her."

"Where were you meeting?"

"Slips my mind." He swung her around, kissed her
hair. "I hope she ate wherever it was."

"Stephen, that's awful."

"Whoever she was."

They all linked arms.

"You made it up."

Emily broke away, ran down Fifty-second Street in front of them, and swung round and round a bus stop, her arms straight out, her body whirling like a propeller.

Stephen caught her, and she fell against him.

"I'm soo dizzy."

"I should think you would be."

"Stephen"—she made a dead weight in his arms— "you will simply have to carry me. I'm too dizzy."

"You're also too large for me to carry."

"That's imaginary," she whispered, out of breath. "My size is entirely imaginary. I'm really very small and you'll have to carry me."

Stephen took her shoulders, put his arms under her legs.

"See," she said triumphantly.

"I am having trouble imagining this Emily," he groaned.

"Concentrate."

"I am." He collapsed against the bus stop, Emily on top of him. "It just doesn't work." And they both laughed.

"Mama," Pia said, concerned. "People are going to think you're crazy."

"You're right, Pia." She stood, pulled Stephen up with her. "People will think we're crazy, Stephen."

They marched earnestly up Fifty-second Street arm in arm.

"It's probably too late to eat tonight," Pia said. "Do you think so?"

"I am afraid it is too late," Stephen said solemnly. "Tomorrow we will eat."

Pia slept with Emily in the rocky double bed at the Gladstone. Stephen slept on the floor beside them.

"Stephen?" Emily called when she heard Pia's breathing deepen to sleep. She reached down, took his hand and fell asleep.

Stephen woke early. A light-and-dust shaft crossed the room, crossed Emily's face, and she was sleeping. It touched him unaccountably to see her there.

He had known the bone-dry survival of early mornings like yesterday in Philadelphia, with that woman, Adela, in bed next to him—had learned to outlast that loneliness mechanically. But this morning surged in him with new life as morning ought to do and had not done in him for years. To his astonishment, he wept. He had not been moved to weep since Belfast, on the pulpit, and after that he had left Ireland, with a hard thickened mollusk shell, prepared for an America where people can more easily live loose-end, untextured lives. Untouched.

February 1956. The rain was gentle, the air warmer than was common in February. He put on his habit for the last time, to face his congregation, the hard, worn faces of workingmen who daily went to factories, lived without the sun, railed silent against the near, constant dreariness of their daily lives, sitting now in timeworn tweeds, patched at the elbow, with their timeworn

Gaelic wives, to worship the Lord through Stephen Williamson, the solid comfortable graceful presence of Stephen Williamson, whom they had known since he was a boy tossing two pennies at Eagen Downs— now gone off to university, a worker's son and come back to his roots. His people.

He had a talk prepared for them. Had written it twelve times—it was all wrong—about Margaret and how he could not be a minister of God any longer and had to leave the West End and Belfast for good. He knew it was all wrong when he got in the pulpit and looked down on those faces as familiar as his father's face, as his own now-weathered face in the looking-glass.

"No good," he said, and tossed the papers he had worked on for days. He walked down the steps and into the congregation, starting in the front row, embracing them each by each row by row, to the end of the church, full as usual on Sunday.

"Elizabeth," he said into the older woman's ear. She gripped his hand.

"And John. Now you've got to stay out of the pub on Saturday," he said. "Will be the death of you . . .

"Good-bye, Mitchell. You're a good man but plainly too fat," he said, his voice shaking.

"I'll be back, Addie," he whispered to one woman old not in years but troubles. "Ireland's a place for old men. You said yourself."

And then his own father come to church to hear his son's last sermon and now no sermon to hear. He shook his father's hand, and the stiff and toughened man who'd send him quivering to his room when he was a boy gripped his son in both his arms.

He went to his office then, shut the door, listened to

the hollow patter of shoes against the church stone floor
and wept.

"Stephen?" Emily looked down at him curiously.

"I don't know what's got into me," he said.

She slid off the bed, down next to him.

"Are you well?"

"I'm very well," he said. "Better than I've been for
some time. But starved. We forgot to eat last night."

Chapter Nine

"Iт's so нот," Pia whispered, burying her head under the cane seat of the canoe.

"Hush." Stephen raised his hand for quiet.

"Stephen has a fish," Emily said.

"A big one," Stephen said.

"It's been nearly four hours." Pia wound her braids over her eyes. "We should have a fish by now."

"This one will make up for the others." Stephen pulled at his line, brought in a river bass. It was not a big one. "So there. You see," he said triumphantly. He slapped it down on the bottom of the canoe; it flipped and straightened like a rubber band, then settled flat.

"Dead?"

"Mmm." Stephen looked at the fish eye to eye. "Nearly."

"It's ugly. Mama?"

Emily leaned against the stern, her eyes closed to the sun.

"Did ya see Stephen's fish?"

She looked up slightly—"Mmm,"—closed her eyes again. "Lovely fish, Stephen."

"Take a good look. This is a fine fish."

"Better be. It's nearly lunchtime."

"Ten-thirty."

"But we've been here since six."

"You've no patience, Pia," Stephen said. "You'll make a very poor wife."

"I don't think I want to be a wife," Pia said, pulling the fish slightly by the tail; it snapped up just at the nose, then flopped back with a hollow thud against the ribs. "I want to be a veterinarian," and then, "My mother might want to be a wife." She tried to be nonchalant.

"Oh?" Stephen grabbed Emily around the waist. "That's not what she's told me."

"No, Stephen," Emily squealed. "Don't."

He rolled her with one quick movement over the side of the canoe. The water, warm in early October, sloshed over her head and, suddenly awake from the long morning, mellow in the sun, she swam through the river out of reach.

"Stay in the canoe, Pia," Stephen called, diving into the water after Emily, "in case you have to save us." He swam swiftly underwater, dark murky water, the Delaware, hard to see in, but close on he saw her long legs, spread them open and came up kissing her underwater on the breasts and stomach.

"Stephen," she whispered when he had surfaced. "Pia."

"Pia couldn't see a battleship in this water." He wrapped his legs around her.

"Tastes like oil." She made a face. "Think we'll die of rotten water?"

"Likely." With his legs, he drew her under, kissed her on the lips. She slid away from him, beneath his arms, swam back to the canoe.

"You'll tip it over, Mama," Pia said, as Emily pulled herself up by the arms over the gunwale of the canoe.

Stephen came up on the other side. "We have to pull at the same time so the ship won't tip, love."

Emily grabbed his arms across from her. "Ready?"

"Ready."

"Pull." They pulled, Emily scrambling, kicking her long legs against the tilt of the boat away from her towards the heavier body of Stephen.

"Watch the fish," Stephen shouted, feeling the boat heaving over on him. "Whatever you do, Pia, hold onto the blessed fish."

Pia grabbed onto the river bass. "It's so slimy," she squeaked. Emily dropped back off the other side of the boat, and Pia, gripping the slippery bass, fell backwards into the water; going under, the bass in her arms popped through the circle of her arms as though they were oiled.

"Gone," she cried, surfacing. Stephen was holding onto the upside-down canoe.

"Bloody fish." He dove over where Pia had surfaced. "Get the boat, Emily." Emily took the small rope and started to swim the short distance to shore, the upturned canoe trailing behind her. Pia pushed from the other end.

"Aha," Stephen shouted, coming above water again. "Got her." And he climbed up on the bank holding the bass.

"There now," he said, pulling the canoe up with Emily, emptying the last of the water that had filled the shell. "Wasn't that a lovely morning, and look what we've got to show for it."

Emily laughed. Shook out her hair.

"What?" Pia asked in consternation.

"Lunch."

"Lunch?" Pia stormed off down the path ahead of them. "I won't eat that fish," she announced self-righteously. "I saw him alive."

It was early October, warm with an aging summer sun, a yellow dryness in the air that left the day early with a surprise chill. Stephen had been with Emily for six weeks. He moved into the small row house on Pine Street a few days after her opening in New York, bringing some clothes with him and a small oil painting of Ireland—one he had painted quite badly himself.

"You don't mind?" he asked Emily formally about the painting.

"Of course not."

"I've always had it," he said apologetically. "I know it's dreadful, but it's just something I've always had."

"Don't be silly."

"I have a bear I've always had all my life," Pia said from the center of her mother's bed where she was watching the proceedings. "His name is Alfred and he's lost an ear."

"Perhaps it doesn't go with the decoration."

"I have no decoration." Emily laughed. "You are embarrassed, Stephen. Here." She took the painting, hung it on the wall beside the bed under one of hers. "Okay?"

She gave him half her dresser, the top half for his shirts and sweaters, cleared out her closet and moved her things into Pia's room. She had never cleared out her drawer for a guest before.

"Pia and I have very little," she explained. "We can easily share a closet."

"Have you come to stay long?" Pia asked when Stephen finished putting away his socks and sat down.

"Perhaps," he said. "For a while at least."

He took out a cigar.

"Stephen says he only smokes when he's having a good time," she explained to her mother.

"I see."

"You don't like smoking," he said. "I'm sorry." He put the cigar back in his pocket.

"That's all right. You can smoke."

"No," he said. "No, I wouldn't. You're quite right. It is awful in the bedroom." He put his arms behind his head. "I have lived alone for nearly ten years. You may find me disagreeable."

Initially they were like that with each other—careful, apologetic, even formal.

"D'you think you might stay forever?" Pia went on.

"Forever?"

"Live here with us forever."

"That's a very long time, Pia. Forever."

"Well, if you decided to, you could have my room. It's the best room." Pia pretended to take a splinter out of her bare foot. "That is, if you wanted to have your own room."

"That's kind of you, Pia. I will think about it when the time comes."

The time had come. Early October. They had planned a weekend in Bucks County. Stephen had picked Pia up at school after his two o'clock lecture on Friday and they had gone to New York to meet Emily in her last day of filming a new series of "Better Promises." They sat on folded metal chairs in the studio waiting for the final episode to be filmed—Emily painted rosy in a Sears, Roebuck housedress, her hair done in a bun that flopped and fell, slid down in the stage sofa, put her arms over her eyes and sighed, "Let's hurry up," so even Stephen and Pia, half-sleeping on Stephen's arm, could hear her.

"Damn it, Laura," a man in front of the set said. "Can't someone back there fix your hair so it'll stay in place for ten minutes?"

"I don't know."

Andy Brown, the town lawyer, the man down the street in "Better Promises," hot on Laura now because she knew that Andy's wife, Prudence, was interested in another man and Andy knew too but didn't know who it might be unless it was Jay Enders who ran the filling station or Dr. Barter, the local obstetrician, who made a regular practice of women and had an advantage.

"Emily's tired," Andy said.

"Emily's tired," the film director, called Bilbo, mocked. "Well, Emily, are you so tired that you want to go back to Philly and screw the rest of this episode?"

Emily shrugged, walked off the set without replying.

"Women," Bilbo said. "I can't stand to work with women. They give me ulcers."

When she came back, her hair was done in a precise bun, her housedress pressed and she was carrying roses in a vase.

"Ready," she said.

"Okay, Andy," Bilbo called, full of spirit now. "Get off the couch."

Andy moved off the set.

"Ready," he called to the camera crew. "Ready."

The doorbell rang.

Laura Rand walked across the room, set down the vase of roses on a table, turned slightly facing the camera.

"Come in," she called. "It's open."

"Laura." Andy Brown came through the door.

"Hello, Andy."

"Laura." He kissed her on the cheek. She moved away, put her hand to her cheek. "Don't, Laura. I mean it."

"I'm sorry, Andy. It's just that I don't have so much trust in men since Dr. Barter."

"And you shouldn't. He was terrible to you."

"I guess I asked for it."

"It's just such a shame, Laura, you living here all alone, lovely as you are."

She brightened. Smiled. "Oh, thank you, Andy."

"It is. I was thinking that this morning to myself. There's Laura Rand, nicer to people than the minister's wife, and just as pretty as a picture. Some lucky man's going to marry her someday."

"Doesn't seem to be happening very rapidly." Laura sat down on the couch, patted the seat next to her for Andy. "You got troubles, Andy?"

Andy paced the floor. "Not real troubles, Laura." He walked over to Laura, took her face in his hands. "You tell me, Laura Rand, do I have troubles?"

"Why, Andy, I don't know." She fussed with her skirt. "I just don't know. You looked a little down and out when you came in."

"I got troubles all right, Laura," he said, and the music began to play, the low, slow theme song of

"Better Promises," "and you know all about them." The lights on the set dimmed; Emily took off her shoes and went out the stage door.

"Okay, Laura." Bilbo sighed. "Back to Philly with your boyfriend."

"This is a hard way to make money," Stephen said to Pia. "Is he always so unpleasant?"

"He's new," Pia answered. "I never saw him before."

"I don't like the way he is to your mother."

"He's very mean," Pia agreed, and then later, as they were leaving the studio, "Do you love my mother?"

"I could."

"D'you think you'll ever marry her?"

"I don't know." He took her hand, walked down the back stairs of the studio to the lobby, where they were to meet Emily. "Do you think she'd agree to that?"

Pia considered. "Maybe." And then, just as they saw Emily get off the elevator, "But maybe not too. She's funny about getting married."

At dinner in the Lumberville Inn in Bucks County, where they went for the weekend after the filming, Stephen asked Emily himself, sitting with her over wine in a quiet corner of the inn.

"Pia asked today if I was going to marry you."

"Oh?"

"Well?"

"Are you asking for Pia or yourself?" She leaned over the table and kissed him. "Or are you asking?"

"For Pia, of course."

Emily rested her chin in her hands. "Why do you want to marry?"

"For my old age, Emily. My fast-approaching old age."

"You're not old yet."

"Very nearly. When the creaks come in and my back goes bad and I need tea in bed and stories read to me to sleep. You're young yet, and you will dismiss me when I go to seed unless I've bought you by law."

She laughed and shook her head.

"You won't, will you?"

"Marry?" She moved her chair closer to him, took his hand. "No, I won't."

"What is it in you, Emily?" He finished off his wine.

"I don't know."

"Perhaps I'd do better with a nice fat jolly sensible girl."

"I don't want to marry, Stephen. I just don't," she said. "My parents had a bad marriage."

"Plenty of people marry quite satisfactorily whose parents have had a bad marriage."

"It's more than that," she said. "Something in the way I am. It would turn sour, that's all."

He looked at her, disbelieving.

"And worse," she added.

"What do you mean?"

"I have fallen in love," she said. "I never thought I could do that without cracking apart and I haven't cracked apart yet."

"You're a peculiar woman." Stephen kissed her lightly on the head. "Trouble is, you make it very difficult for me to be interested in fat jolly sensible girls."

Emily woke Stephen from a sound sleep in the middle of the night.

"I can't sleep," she said, moving into his arms.

"Sorry," he groaned. "I was not having much trouble myself."

"I know," she whispered. "I hate to wake you, but I've had this awful headache come on sudden so I couldn't think."

He rubbed her head. She moved right next to him, relaxed in his arms.

"Stephen."

"Yes."

"Let's not talk about marriage."

"I didn't know we were. In fact, I thought we were sleeping."

"You know what I mean."

"It won't come up again."

Perhaps, he thought, before falling back to sleep, the time would not come between them for more than a peripheral commitment, circumscribed life, a moment vital of itself but without future, without possibilities. They were both too careful—ultimately too careful. But surely it had not been careful to fall in love.

When he awoke to the alarm before dawn, she was awake already, kissing his lips, rubbing her fingers through his hair.

"We're going fishing. Remember?" she said.

"What time is it?"

"Five." She kissed him hard. "It was your idea to get up at five."

Stephen left the fish he'd caught in the picnic basket and ran up the wooded path above the river.

"First up the tree," he shouted behind him and scrambled up a low strong oak with patches of yellow and blue amidst the thick leaves.

"I can't," Emily said, struggling to pull herself up, straining her arms.

"Here." Stephen reached down. "Give me a hand."

"Lord," he groaned. "You are heavy."

"Oh." Emily fell across the top branch, pulled herself up beside him. "Hold me," she shouted. "I'm going to fall."

"You're surely not the warrior type, are you?"

"I used to spend gym class in the bathroom," she said, her hand gripping his, unsteady.

"Now look, love, if you hold on to me, we'll both go down." He pushed his back against the trunk. "Will Pia be all right going off alone?"

"She'll be fine. She goes on walks alone lots."

"I wonder if she'll forgive me killing that fish?"

"She'll recover." She wrapped her legs around the branch. "Stephen." She tilted her head back so he could hear her more easily. "Are we here because you think it's romantic to be up in a tree?"

"Don't you think it's romantic?"

"No."

He grabbed her around the waist, kissed her neck.

"Stephen." She slipped off the branch, held tight with her arms.

"You are hopeless, Emily."

She let go and dropped to the ground.

"I don't find it romantic," she said. "Just uncomfortable."

He dropped down beside her.

"Will Pia be gone long?"

"A while."

"Can we count on it?" He kissed her nose. "Come."
He crawled under low brush, moving some of the way
on his stomach beneath a jungle of bushes and vines;
she followed him. He made her a pillow of dry leaves
and they lay on their backs looking up at the noonday
sun filtered through the heavy leaves, the finer low
brush and spider vines, a fine web of line and color,
gentle sun twice broken, scattered in small patterns
above them. She took off her smock.

"You have no shame, Emily Fielding."

She laughed, lifted his shirt, kissed him on the breast
and they lay against the gentle crack of autumn dry
leaves beneath them.

"Tell me about your wife," she asked. "Do you think
of her when you make love to me?"

"I have," he said. "Once or twice. She was a plain
woman, simple and fresh. You would have liked her."

"Was she like me?"

"Not at all. Perhaps now, if I met her now, I wouldn't
fall in love with her. But she was right for me at that
time when we were young."

"Is it the same to fall in love with me?" She giggled,
low and gentle. "You have, you know."

"I suppose I have," he said. "It's not the same. I fell
in love with Margaret slowly, over years, from a time
when I was quite small. With you it has been different
altogether. Stunning."

"Aren't you afraid?"

"What do you mean?"

"To have gone ten years without falling in love with
anyone. Either you are afraid or very careful."

"Next to you, my love, I'm very careless."

"I'm so self-protective?"

"Bloody hell, Emily. You're like an armadillo." He kissed her. "We'd better go. Sure Pia will be back soon."

Fact was, she was afraid. She had taken great care with the order of her life, that its patterns be under her control, that it not strain beyond her capacity to know, and now this new space, she struggled to understand, this sense of flying above the trees, wingless, too far from earth knowing surely there were air pockets along the way, funneling to a sharp drop against an asphalt surface, but it was too splendid to give up the sense of flying. She was afraid, surely and with good reason, as she knew. But she was in love too.

Pia was reading the paper when Emily and Stephen came down from the woods. The wedding section of the *Times.*

"Pia always reads the weddings," Emily said as they approached. "She likes to read what the bride wore and her attendants."

"Pia is very interested in the general subject of weddings, it seems."

Emily frowned. "Not mine," she said. "It's fairy godmothers and beautiful princesses that she likes."

"Listen, Mama." Pia was turned on her stomach, chin in hands. " 'Miss Roosevelt wore her great-grandmother's silk and lace dress fashioned with leg-of-mutton sleeves.' What's that?"

"Lord, child." Stephen took out his fish, spread out the financial section under the fish and slit it down the center.

"It looks awful." Pia hid her eyes. "I won't eat it. There was a flower girl too. 'Miss Eleana Roosevelt, the bride's cousin, wore a white organdy dress which had been her grandmother's when she was a child.' " She flipped back several pages. "When I get married, I want an enormous wedding with a trumpet. There was a trumpet at that wedding."

Emily spread out a blanket, opened the picnic basket, took out the wine.

"Wine, Stephen?" He drank it.

"Hot."

"C'n I?" Pia asked.

Emily gave Pia some wine in a small cup.

"There," she said, kissing her forehead. "In celebration of your approaching wedding."

"Well," Pia said seriously. "It's not really approaching. I don't even know who I want to marry."

"That we can figure out easily enough," Stephen said, blowing the fire to catch on the larger wood. "The problem to consider is the wedding anyway."

"Pia, turn back a page, will you?" Emily peered over her shoulder. Something had caught her eye.

"To the weddings?"

"No, the obituaries."

She corked the wine, sat back on her heels.

"I read the obituaries," Stephen said, salting the frying pan. "Plotting my chances."

Emily wrinkled her brow. "There," she said.

Pia stopped turning.

Lydia Biddle Fowler, of Philadelphia: Lydia Fowler, youngest daughter of the late Anthony Biddle, noted financier, died Friday morning at Bryn Mawr Hospital in Bryn Mawr, Pennsylvania. Mrs. Fowler, also

the wife of Henry Fowler, was a noted philanthro-
pist, active in the building of Bryn Mawr Hospital,
the south wing of which is named in her honor, and
past local president of the Florence Crittenden
Homes. In 1949 and 1953, she won first prize at the
Philadelphia Flower Show for her tea garden roses.
She leaves, besides her husband, four grandchildren.
Her only child, Jane Fielding, died in 1956.

"My grandmother?" Pia asked

"My grandmother," Emily said.

"We've never seen her."

"You've never seen her."

Stephen stood up, looked over their heads at the paper.

"Your mother's mother?" He knelt down and read. Emily had not mentioned her family to Stephen before. He hadn't inquired; he seldom mentioned his own family, although he thought about them—sometimes early in the morning he would wake up before dawn with the smell of his mother in the room and a heavy-headedness would press down on him. But he did not talk about them to Emily because he had left Belfast behind, and even now had not sorted out his memories about them.

With Emily, there was an intentional avoidance, and now, with her family on page 36 of the New York *Times*, he sensed in her a kind of unfamiliar anger.

Once, early on, they had talked about mothers.

"My mother is dead," she had said. "She was beautiful."

"Like you?"

"Not like me at all. I'm not beautiful," she said crossly. "She broke people with her beauty." And that was all she had to say. If she wasn't going to talk about her family, he wasn't going to ask. After all, he spent the best part of his day talking to people about their families. It was agreeable to pretend that Emily had bloomed full grown, untied to any past associations. That they were both rooted only in themselves. It was easy to pretend that in America.

Emily slapped shut the newspaper and spread out plates.

"Are you sad, Mama?"

"I had thought she was immortal."

"Have I told you about my grandmother?" Stephen said to turn the tide. "She made Christmas cookies all year, every Sunday, in the middle of June, tiny little bells and trees. Even the year my father was out of work and there was plain beans and potatoes to eat, there she would be fussing in the kitchen with her bells and trees, him steaming at her full of rancor, saying she was damned crazy to be using sugar and butter for Christmas cookies in June." He flipped the fish in the pan. "But I don't think she was crazy at all." He served Emily and himself. "Still won't try any of this lovely fish, Pia?"

"Nope."

"Poor fish, you'll hurt his feelings. Turning him down like this."

"Really?" Pia looked up, frowning.

"I'm sure you will."

"Well . . . Mama?"

"Pia, I know nothing of the feelings of a fish."

"You've got to be extra sensitive to know about fish feelings, Pia."

"Just a little, then." She held out her plate. "You're sure he won't care?"

"Absolutely."

"Are we going to see your grandmother now she's dead?" Pia asked.

"I think not."

"I have never gotten to see anyone dead. Is it terrible?"

"Will you go to the funeral?" Stephen asked.

"No." Emily was pensive. "I really haven't seen her for years, not since my mother died."

"Your family dies a lot," Pia said.

"My mother was murdered, Pia. I told you that," Emily said, taking another glass of wine. "Otherwise she would have lived forever. And my grandmother was eighty, I'm sure."

"That's awful, isn't it? Murdered," Pia said with a certain delight. "Are you scared of the dark, Stephen?"

"No, Pia, I'm more scared of the light," Stephen said. "Is that right, Emily? You never told me."

She nodded.

"I think I'll go see my grandfather, though." She changed the subject. "This evening after we get home. Poor man. How long he's had to wait."

Later, Stephen came over to Emily, who was resting by a tree, her eyes closed.

"I think I'm drunk," she said. "Every time I open my eyes, things whirl around."

"You must be, then." He lay down in the grass beside her, took her hand, held it next to his face.

"What's wrong?"

"I've been irresponsible," she said. "I ought to have known better."

"Getting drunk?"

"I don't know." She closed her eyes tight against the spinning trees, the bright kaleidoscope of autumn. "Falling in love, I guess."

Chapter Ten

"**I** WOULD LIKE to see Mr. Fowler," Emily said. She and Stephen stood at the impressive entrance of her grandparents' home in Gladwyne. It was a quiet and imposing home, like many of the Main Line homes built at the turn of the century in the American lust for a gilded age, now mellow with time and grand in a kind of distinguished and admirable way that belied the creeping decadence within.

"Mr. Fowler is unavailable." The black lady in uniform was self-possessed and distant, trained in demeanor no doubt by Lydia Fowler.

"I am his granddaughter."

Behind the black lady was another lady, in a nurse's uniform. Starched and efficient, she was snapping through the dark and enormous entrance hall.

"It is Mr. Fowler's granddaughter," the black lady said. "She would like to see him."

The nurse looked up from the tray of bottles that she was carrying.

"Impossible," she said, and then halfway across the hall her curiosity got the better of her efficiency and she marched back past the black lady at the door and met Emily face to face.

"Granddaughter?" she asked fiercely.

"Yes," Emily said.

"I didn't know he had children."

"He had one child," Emily said. "My mother who is dead."

The nurse arched her eyebrows above the steel-rimmed glasses flattened against her plump brow.

"Well," she said. "He is not in good form. Bereaved," she added forcefully.

Emily could not imagine.

"But I will check his blood pressure and mention to him that you are here." She clattered back across the hall. "Don't count on it," she added, mindful of her authority.

The black lady in uniform stepped back to let Stephen and Emily pass through.

"There's many here already," she said in a surprising flow of conversation. "Go through the dining room to the study. There is food as well." She bounced after them. "You may see some that you know. Everyone's here."

Emily passed through the entrance hall to the dining room. The long, polished table was still there with a silver bowl of fresh flowers from the garden and candelabra—years since they'd eaten there perhaps, but still fresh flowers in the centerpiece as there had always been, as if the family dined there every night. And the table as long as Emily remembered it with the high-back chairs, tapestry thrones. Emily ran her finger along the table as they walked through and collected no dust.

The study was full of people. A bar was open and there was an array of food, of hams and turkeys spread on a lowboy, as if they had waited these months sitting brown and fat in the larder ready for Lydia Fowler to die. There was her grandfather's desk, where she had sat and crayoned, cut paper dolls those long years of the war.

"Henry," Lydia Fowler would call, her voice slicing sharply through the house. "Have you seen Emily?"

"No, m'dear," he would call, giving Emily a wink. "She might be out in the garden."

"Jane and I are going shopping and Emily must have a Sunday coat." During the war years, Emily was the only child at Sunday School who had both a Sunday and weekday coat.

Above the desk was a picture of Lydia Fowler with her only daughter. A soft French garden picture, typical of the time, done in pale oils—Lydia Fowler seated on a chair in a long dress with lace high under her chin, straight chin sharp as a needle, a face as cold and neatly made as if it had been cast from memory by a minor artist who had studied the perfect human form. And Jane Fowler, dark as Egypt, like the Fowlers, leaning against her mother's knee in high-top shoes—dark like Pia, Emily realized, with Pia's black hair and startled eyes. Jane Fowler of Philadelphia—Jane Fowler Fielding, lately of Washington—bound and trussed, tossed in the Potomac River. And suddenly Jane Fowler was back with Emily, alive and masterful as she had remembered her in this very study when Emily was six years old.

One Sunday she and her grandfather had been walking back from the meadow, where they had gone to make clover chains—that's the sort of thing he could do with Emily—hours on end—when a terrible racket like a cat fight broke out on the porch.

"Back to the prison with us, Em," her grandfather said.

"Back to the prison with us," Emily repeated. It was their password, and every time they returned from the woods or the garden to Lydia Fowler's domain, they shared the same exchange.

"Grandmother's fighting with Mother," Emily said as they got closer to the porch and could hear the brittle voices back and forth.

"So she is," her grandfather had said. "I think we'll go round the side door by the study. There." He put the clover chain he had just finished over her head. "You look lovely."

As they passed the porch, Emily saw Anthony Call and her mother standing in a corner of the porch; she didn't see her grandmother.

When they entered the study, her grandmother was there, blue with anger.

"Henry." She shut the door to the study. "Jane has been indiscreet."

"That is no revelation, Lydia."

"With Anthony Call," she said in a harsh whisper. "Emily, you will have to leave." But she went on even though Emily simply retreated behind her grandfather. "Whose father ran a meat market on Lancaster Pike, as I recall."

"Are you concerned about Jane's indiscretion or Mr. Call's lineage?"

"Henry," she began, but at that moment a raging Jane Fielding burst into the room, slammed shut the door and slapped her mother on the face.

In seconds, it seemed, Anthony Call sped out of the

driveway in his old yellow car, Jane Fielding beside him.

"Henry."

Her grandfather had sat down at his desk, pulled Emily onto his lap.

"Henry," she said, leaning over his desk. "Are you going to do nothing?"

He played with Emily's clover chain.

"You are going to do nothing," she said fiercely. "It is a remarkable aspect of your character, Henry, that given any extreme situation you manage consistently to do nothing."

When she had left, he locked the study door.

The starched nurse tapped Emily on the arm.

"Mr. Fowler will see you now," she said.

"I'll be back soon," she whispered to Stephen.

"But you may only stay a short time," the nurse cautioned.

Stephen wandered amongst the food tables, drank a bourbon intended for someone else offered him by accident, sat on the edge of the couch and watched the people. The people at this party, for surely it was a party, one of the many at which the same people, mostly elderly, assembled several times a year, by the general tenor of conversation, the sense of formal intimacy, and Stephen supposed that parties after funerals had replaced the cocktail parties of their middle years, the weddings and debutante parties of their youth—these were all people who had known each other all their lives, no doubt, who had shared in each other's ceremonies as a condition of their being, and it struck him

how little of this world to which Emily certainly by
blood belonged he understood.

They had parties like this in Belfast. When his grandmother who made Christmas cookies all year long had
died, they had an enormous party at his father's house—
his grandmother laid out in a nightgown, right in the
living room next to the couch—but theirs was a party
full of passion, not ordered and unpresuming as this
cold-blooded celebration.

His mother, working-class Catholic, fiery, charming,
impractical, had married his father, a God-fearing, re-
pressed Protestant worker who was already an old man
at eighteen when they married—and their union set
loose such a range of feelings on the Catholic side and
stiff reprisals on the Protestant side that the marriage
lasted solid as granite for the sheer turbulence that it
created around them. Until Grandmother O'Leary
moved in with her Christmas cookies and under-the-
table snorts of pure sherry (nondrinking Protestants, the
Williamsons, of the worst sort), and her going to 6:00
A.M. Mass on purpose every morning, when all the
Protestants in the West End were up to work at 6:00
A.M., so they saw Mrs. O'Leary, a square of black lace on
her pale red hair, lumbering down to the Catholic
church. They gave it strong to Ronald Williamson at
work, harboring Catholics in his own home—and then
to the shame of all the Williamsons, Mrs. O'Leary dying
(of a prune seed in her stomach, so she said, which
grow'd big as a watermelon until she burst) and having
a regular Catholic wake right in the Williamsons' living
room with all the O'Leary drunken brothers, bleary-
eyed from weeping over their poor dear sister, so they

said, but sure it was they were bleary-eyed from drinking, and late in the evening, Michael O'Leary, so drunk he could not find the casket to give a speech for the dear departed Bernadette, and, finding it at last, fell into it atop his dead sister.

"Adine Williamson," Stephen's father had called to his mother when it happened (all the children giggling like fools in the corner of the room to see a drunk and living man fallen in a casket). His mother was in the kitchen bringing out the cakes the neighbors brought (the neighbors brought themselves as well, presumably to pay respects to the dead—grim Protestants all with a certain morbid curiosity about a Catholic wake, to see these blustering intemperate people in festival mood and condemn them and laugh at straight-armed Ronald Williamson for having to put up with the likes of Catholic blood he'd been sure fool enough to marry into).

"Adine."

She appeared in the doorway with a plate of cakes.

"Oh, God." She set down the cakes on the table and rushed over to the casket.

"Uncle Michael." She pulled on his shoulders. "Timothy," she called to her brother who was in the corner of the room telling an improper joke to the younger children. Timothy couldn't be counted on for much, but he was strong.

"You've got to help me."

Timothy lifted Michael by the shoulders.

"Mother of God," he said. Michael was dead weight—dead asleep.

Two other brothers came over; Ronald Williamson, white-faced and stiff, stood in the center of the room and did not move to leave or help his wife remove her uncle from the casket.

"You men take his legs." Two uncles dutifully took Michael's legs and Timothy took his arms. "Heave ho." They lifted—one uncle, not much more sober than Michael, fell with one of Michael's legs.

"Put him on my bed," Adine said. "Put them both on my bed." She indicated the other uncle on the floor holding Michael's leg. "And shut the door."

"Poor chap," the uncle on the floor said. "Old Michael so loved his sister that he thought he'd be buried with her," and they all, the O'Learys all but Adine, drank a toast to poor Michael and then to Bernadette and then to the good Ronald Williamson, who left the house and took a long walk on the Common.

When Grandmother O'Leary was laid to her final rest (as good a woman as ever there was save for the Virgin Mary, so the priest said), the Williamson household repaired itself. Straightened. The days became longer and duller without Grandmother O'Leary, but even with the tedious Protestant God and Ronald Williamson's suffering sobriety, there was more life in Stephen's house than in this one where Emily had started her days.

Emily had never been in her grandparents' living quarters or, if she had, she did not remember, and walking the long corridor now, it seemed to her as if no one had been in these quarters for forty years. They smelled wasted and of death. Her grandfather's room was at the back of the house with tiers of lead pane windows overlooking the garden. The age and mustiness of the room, the large canopied bed with a crocheted coverlet, kept it from seeming medicinal in spite of the efforts of the efficient nurse.

Henry Fowler sat in an overstuffed chair, like a china-headed doll with jointed legs and arms of plaster, a diminished Henry Fowler wrapped in a stadium blanket; his fingers laced together like fine thread.

"Grandfather," Emily said, kneeling beside him on a footstool: "bless this house—l.b.f. 1921." "It's Emily."

His eyes were wet and painted blue, vacant like glass eyes, a waxed-paper film over the pupil; she wondered if he were blind.

"I don't know an Emily," he said, his voice cracked and dry as though he rarely spoke.

"Your granddaughter. Remember?" She put her warm hand atop his folded ones; he did not flinch.

"Jane's daughter."

"Jane's dead."

"We stayed with you during the war and then moved to Washington. I saw you lots when I was young. Do you remember when you broke your leg and I used to wheel you through the garden?"

"Lydia?" He looked at her then, the first time he had turned his head.

"No, I'm Emily." She did look like Lydia. Everyone had always said so—around the eyes at least, and her nose was surely a Biddle nose.

"You're not Lydia." He seemed to relax then, his hands beneath Emily's sinking deeper in his lap.

Henry Fowler met Lydia at Penn Law School, where her father occasionally taught and he, the first child in his family to receive an education, struggling through school on odd jobs, fell immediately in love with this maiden of the season, the lovely, wealthy Lydia Biddle, back from Paris at nineteen. They married in 1908 when he finished at Penn and for eight glorious months he had a proper job as a Philadelphia lawyer and lived in a cozy house on First Street with his bride. Then the senior Biddle had died, Lydia inherited Tredifferin, the family country home on the Main Line, and the fortune, vast for that time, amassed by her grandfather.

"You cannot work," she had told Henry. "There is too much to do managing the house and father's money for you to work. Besides," she had added, "you needn't." And she made him utterly grateful for that during the rest of his life. Henry Fowler saved them in the Crash, saw it coming and took his money out of investments, but that was the only accomplishment of his working career. By the time he was forty, he had turned the books over to an accountant and spent most of his time in the garden. He even stopped reading the paper except on Sundays, and when Emily knew him best, he was a rather simple man with a child's mind and pleasures and a spirit as generous as the bounty of flowers from his garden.

"You Biddle women destroy the men you live with," Emily's own father had shouted during one of the fights he had had with Jane Fielding right before her death. "And I don't want to end up like Henry Fowler."

"When I lived here with you, we used to read books in your study," Emily said. "I'd sit on your lap. It was very large like a chair and you had whiskers then that went like this." She pulled down on her skin imitating his whiskers. He was listening, she could tell. There was a certain perkiness about him. "They scratched my cheeks something awful. We would hide from Mother and Grandmother, from all the chores they wanted us to do, the places they wanted us to go."

"Lydia's dead, you know," he cracked. "Died in the night."

"And you remember Sunday dinners?" she dared, pressing his bone hand tight. "At the long table with you at one end and Lydia at the other. Jane and Lydia would have terrible fights and make dinner unbearable."

The old man brightened visibly; his eyes seemed clearer.

"Do you remember before dinner, we'd go through the garden hand in hand? You'd show me how you'd transplanted or spliced or pruned and then we'd go into the woods and you'd listen to all my foolish child's stories. We'd walk and walk until my poor legs nearly folded."

"Back to the prison with us, Em," he said in his dry, cracked voice. "Back to the prison."

"You do remember." Emily took both of his hands. "It was a nice time we had together."

"Emily." He almost seemed to smile, his wizened lips like crushed paper. "You're Emily." He squinted his eyes as if he were trying to see her better through the narrow crooked slits. "You have a nice voice," he said. "Soft." They sat together, Emily holding his hands, his head settling back against the pillows, his eyes beginning to close.

"Lydia's dead, you know."

"I know," she said. "She died in the night."

"That's right." Henry Fowler nodded. "She died in the night."

Sixty years must have seemed a long time to wait for that. And not much he could do with it now. Emily waited until he was asleep and then she left.

"You see," the nurse said triumphantly at the door. "He doesn't even know you." She moved to let Emily pass. "He doesn't know anyone but me."

Stephen was standing at the front door.

"I can see you're ready."

"Are you?" He took her hand.

"I am." They walked quickly to the car.

"Was it okay?"

"I'm glad I came."

"How was your grandfather?"

"Victorious." She stepped into the front seat. "He has outlived her."

Stephen got in beside her and pulled out of the long driveway.

"There's an inn up the road in Gladwyne; could we stop for supper?"

"Fine," Stephen said. "If Pia's okay."

"I told the Burroughses we might be late."

She settled back into the seat and took Stephen's hand. It felt ample and thick after her grandfather's hand, full of crisp young hair and usefulness.

"I love you," she said quietly, resting her head against his shoulder.

I I

PIA HAD NOT LIKED the Burroughses since the day two years ago they moved into the house next door in West Philadelphia and Mrs. Burroughs told Amy Burroughs, whom Pia disliked particularly, not to play with Pia until Mrs. Burroughs found out more about her. What with there being no father and Emily being on TV Pia might be a bad influence—straightaway, Amy had told Pia, which started things off on a bad foot. Amy was dull and priggish, more an antique spinster lady than a little girl sitting on her back porch in a rocking chair doing sewing cards. Mr. Burroughs owned houses and rented them out ("Cheap to friends and dear to niggers," so Mr. LaVine around the corner told Emily) and Mrs. Burroughs did Good Works, of her own choosing, mind—she didn't waste much time doing Good Works for her family or her neighbors (that Mr. La-Vine said too; he heard it from Mr. Burroughs, who couldn't stand his wife but told Mr. LaVine not to breathe a word of it to a soul; Mr. LaVine, it was well known, didn't keep a confidence a minute).

But everybody was away on Sunday when Stephen and Emily drove back from Bucks County except the Burroughses, who were always in ("With good reason," Pia said. "Nobody'd invite them out"), so Emily said it would be best for Pia to stay with Amy Burroughs while she went to the Main Line with Stephen to see her grandfather.

Pia lay on her back with her feet on the Burroughses' porch steps and her eyes in the sun. Amy sat in the rocking chair.

"Well," she sighed. "What d'ya want to do?"

"We could make a cake or cookies or something," Pia suggested, shading her eyes with her hands.

"My mother doesn't allow us to make cakes or anything," Amy said. "Says we dirty up the kitchen. Even Buster can't."

Well, it was no wonder that Buster couldn't. Buster was fifteen, and just last week had told Pia he'd give her a quarter if she'd pull down her pants, so it certainly wasn't a good idea to let Buster make a cake or anything else.

"We could jump rope."

"I *hate* to jump rope."

"Or go for a walk down to Thirty-eighth, maybe."

Amy slid down in the chair glumly. "How long's your mother gonna be gone?"

"Two weeks," Pia replied evenly.

"Two weeks!" Amy snapped. "Y'mean you're staying with us for two weeks? My mother said you'd only be here through dinner."

"Maybe a month." Pia closed the sun out of her eyes with her arm. "We can go to Mr. LaVine's." She sat up, brushed the dirt off her shirt. "He always tells a good story or gives me some brownies."

"Mr. LaVine? Is he the man who owns the shop on Thirty-ninth?"

"Yes."

"With comics?"

"Yup." She reached into her pocket and took out a quarter. "I think I'll buy two."

"I'm not allowed to read comics."

"You don't want to come?"

Mrs. Burroughs blew out of the house then, in a

flowered dress and flowered hat, her arms full of cookie tins.

"Cookies for the church social," she sang. "Now, Amy, if Buster comes back, you tell him his father wants to see him. I'm just going to run up to the church for forty seconds. You girls stay close by." She flew up the street and Pia watched her until she turned down Thirty-eighth out of sight.

"I'm going to LaVine's."

"I can't."

"That's okay." Pia started off down Pine. "I don't mind going alone."

Amy got up and followed.

"And leave me here by myself?"

"I'll be right back." She looked at Amy oddly. "Your father's at home, isn't he?"

"Yeah." Amy trotted along beside Pia. "The reason why I can't go to LaVine's is partly the comics and partly because he's Jewish."

"Oh, yeah?" Pia said. "Me too."

"You're Jewish?"

"Yup."

"Well." Amy looked confused. "Mother says he cheats her everytime on the food she gets from him." She kept pace with Pia. "You're sure you're Jewish?"

"Positive."

They walked into LaVine's and Pia got a new issue of *Doctor Strange*.

"D'you know Amy Burroughs, Mr. LaVine?"

"I know Amy's papa."

"My papa comes here?"

"Your papa and I are very good friends." He held up two fingers pressed together. "Like this." He reached into one of the glass cases and took out an apple strudel. "There." He gave one to each of them. "For a treat."

"I have another quarter."

"No, no, no, Pia. For a treat."

"Thank you." Pia ate hers and left with Amy, who was still holding her apple strudel carefully in front of her as though it might explode at any moment.

"Aren't you going to eat it?" Pia asked as they walked along Pine Street.

"I don't know." Amy looked worried. "Do you think it's poison?"

"Poison?" Amy had peculiarities she had not even suspected.

"Y'know. Because I said he was Jewish, he might want to get back at me."

"He knows he's Jewish," Pia said. "He's glad."

"Well," Amy said, not at all convinced. "I'm not very hungry."

Mr. Burroughs was on the front porch as they walked up. He was very large, very angry and wasted no time taking Amy by the arm and marching her into the darkened house with a threatening look at Pia not to follow.

Pia heard the slap of the belt through the open windows, the low wail and, even hating Amy Burroughs as she did, she felt remorse for her part in Amy's downfall.

"Amy's not to go to LaVine's," Mr. Burroughs voice boomed from somewhere within the bowels of the house. "You hear?"

Pia nodded.

"You hear?" he shouted again.

"Yes, sir."

Amy came out a few minutes later. She sat on the top porch step and scowled at Pia.

"I'm really sorry," Pia said. "I didn't know you'd get in trouble."

"Didn't hurt," Amy replied. "I can be whipped twenty times with a belt and it doesn't hurt a bit."

Pia folded her comic and put it in her back pocket. Amy moved down to the bottom step, closer to Pia.

"Y'know what my mother and daddy say?" she asked, not pleasantly.

Pia shook her head; she didn't want to know either.

"They say your mama's a whore," she said low under her breath. "Ya know what a whore is?"

Pia nodded. She didn't know what a whore was, but she suspected it was terrible.

"A whore has all kinds of men in bed with her. Y'know about that?"

Pia knew she was going to cry, startled by the sudden violence in Amy Burroughs, who just a short time before was afraid of poisoned strudels.

"You'll never have a father, because your mother's a whore." She puckered up her lips full of saliva and spat a clear stream at Pia Fielding, but Pia was already running over the back fence, up the alley behind the Drummonds' and the Carrs' and over the Aikens' fence into the Clays' yard and then into her own yard. The window to her mother's studio in the back of the house was always open. She crawled in, pulled it shut behind her and locked it.

Once, some time later, she heard voices, the high shrill voice of Mrs. Burroughs and others outside the window, and then they went away.

Pine Street was full of police cars, flashing red circles low in the sky and people gathered on the sidewalk, more than lived on Pine Street or Thirty-ninth.

"What's up?" Stephen moved through the crowd, Emily behind him.

"Little girl lost."

"Maybe kidnapped," one lady said.

"You never know around here," another was saying. "I've told my Gregory, we ought to move out to the suburbs."

Mrs. Burroughs was olive-green in the streetlight, fluttering like a guinea hen on the top step of her porch.

"There, Officer," she very nearly shrieked. "That's her mother."

A policeman came up to Stephen.

"Are you the father?"

"There is no father," Mrs. Burroughs said, close on his heels; and then to Emily, standing with Stephen, "I was gone for forty seconds to take cookies for the church social."

"Forty minutes," Mr. Burroughs on the front porch bellowed. "Long enough for them to go to LaVine's," he spat.

"And when I came back, Pia had disappeared." She pulled Emily over and whispered, "In a temper, so our Amy said."

"Where did she go?" Emily asked. "Did Amy see her?"

"Over that fence is the last the other child saw of her": an officer, next to Emily. "We have combed the immediate neighborhood. These people saw her go over their back fence at about two-thirty."

"Amy said she lost her temper, just flew off and ran

away." Mrs. Burroughs fanned herself with a church program. "No apparent reason. Just a friendly spat like children have."

"I'm going off with the police and dogs, Mom."

"No, indeed, you don't go off with any police and dogs, Buster Burroughs. It's high time you went to bed."

"It's ten o'clock," Buster said.

Stephen moved over with the officers who had brought dogs.

"They need clothes," he said to Emily. "Something for scent."

"I'll go look," Emily said, going up the front steps of her house. "I'll be right back." She let herself in the house, walked through the dark hall into the kitchen and out the kitchen side door to the garage, which she had converted to a studio. With a mother's second sense about her child, she knew Pia had not disappeared. The studio was dark. She stood at the top step to get her bearing.

"Pia," she called.

The shadow of streetlights filtered through the sky-light and outlined the tables, the sink in the center of the room. Pia was crouched in the large cabinet under the sink.

"Mama."

Emily followed her voice, knelt on the floor with her daughter.

"I thought you weren't coming back," she said.

"I have always come back," Emily said gently.

"You said you'd be here by six."

"I told Mrs. Burroughs I might be as late as ten." She held Pia in her arms. "It's ten now. Haven't you heard the police? There are lots of people outside looking for you."

"I heard," Pia whispered. "I was afraid to come out."

"Afraid of what?"

"Afraid for the trouble I'd caused."

Emily stroked her hair.

"Mama?"

"Yes."

"Amy called you a whore."

"Is that why you left?"

"She said it in an evil way." She held her mother around the waist. "Are you?"

"No," Emily said thoughtfully. "I don't believe I am."

"She said I'd never have a father." She was sobbing quietly. "That's not true, either, is it?"

"Pia." Emily shook her head, flooded, off balance after this day in her own past and now this failure to her child.

"Stephen would like to marry you, wouldn't he?"

"He says he would."

"I want you to marry him."

"Pia," Emily began, and then was quiet.

I I I

EMILY GOT UP in the middle of the night with an urgent anger. A fierce pain in the center of her head. Wide-awake, she went into her studio to work on a wire-mesh form she was shaping, but the anger overtook her and she lashed out against the form with such a vengeance she was astonished at her strength. The wire-mesh form was flattened on the floor; she kicked it out of the way and, exhausted, sat down against the center cupboard and fell asleep.

Stephen awoke to a sense of emptiness in the bed next to him and a steady hollow thud in the rooms beyond.

"Emily?" She was gone. He got up. The sound came from downstairs in the kitchen, beyond the kitchen, got louder, more rhythmic as he went downstairs. The kitchen light was on, the door to the studio open and in the night lights from Pine Street that filtered through the studio windows, he could see Emily in her night-gown.

In the empty space at the center of the room was the wire-mesh form for a sculpture and Emily, flinging her body against it like a madwoman, was beating the mesh form flat.

Stephen retreated, went into the black living room and lay down sleepless on the couch. Shortly, the racket stopped. He waited listening for the sound of Emily's bare feet on the steps and hearing nothing, assumed she had fallen asleep.

There was an old man in West End, Belfast, not so very old really, but he looked that way because he never changed his clothes and his back was bent "from looking at the ground for pennies" so everyone said. And he was plain crazy. Called "Crazy Andrew" by the people around West End Common, where Stephen lived. Stephen had heard about Crazy Andrew, but he had never seen him until one morning going to grammar school with his brother, Peter. (Usually Peter rushed out the door so as not to be seen with his younger brother, but this particular morning, he had not made it, and, disgruntled, he trudged along with Stephen. "Just remember," Grandmother O'Leary used to say to Stephen of Peter, "he's two years older, two years duller and two years meaner," which was perfectly true and didn't help a bit.)

They took the shortcut through Beeker Park to school and there sat Crazy Andrew on a park bench rocking a baby carriage—dressed in old tweeds and a worn silk scarf. He stood as he saw them coming, hailed them down as if they were buses.

"Great sport," said Peter gleefully. "You've never seen Crazy Andrew. "We'll have a good time of it."

"How's it going, Andrew?" Peter shouted as though Andrew were deaf as well. "And how's the baby?"

Stephen looked in the worn wicker baby carriage, full to the top of old clothes and blankets, bottles, old books, a mackintosh, a pair of boots and a cooking pan. There was no baby there.

"There's no baby," Stephen said, confused.

"Look, you dummy," Peter said. "Anyone with eyes can see there's a baby."

Stephen looked, but if there was a baby, it certainly wasn't breathing beneath all that junk.

" 'ave you seen Father Dickory, m'boy?" Andrew asked Stephen. "I'm supposed to give seven o'clock Mass and I went to St. Benedict's but it must 'ave been burned down in the night so I 'aven't 'ad breakfast and I've lost Father Dickory."

"Terrible, Andrew," Peter said.

" 'ave you a piece of silver for a bit of breakfast?"

Stephen reached in his pocket for his lunch money, but Peter slapped his hand.

"There, there," Andrew said to the old clothes in his baby carriage. "It'll be all right. Andrew'll get you some food. Terrible, isn't it, a church like that burning down." He shook his head. "My first turn at the Mass since I entered the order." He turned to Peter. " 'ave you a piece of silver for Crazy Andrew?"

"See, Andrew," Peter said with sudden excitement, "over there in that large tree, hanging from a branch. Look, old man. There's a pot of silver."

Andrew brightened.

"G'wan over. Take a look for yourself."

Andrew ran over to the tree.

"See, there it is. Right before your eyes."

"That's cruel, Peter."

"Shut up, he doesn't know the difference," Peter said. "He's plain crazy. We aren't even in the same world, Andrew and the rest of us." He started to run along the path. "Reach for it, Andrew. That's it, old man, you've got it." And he ran far ahead up the path around the bend out of sight.

Stephen didn't run but moved on, and when he did look back, just before the bend in the path, Andrew was back at the bench rocking the carriage, head bent down as though he were sleeping.

"Trouble with you," Peter told him later, "is you haven't a clue how to have a good time of it."

Until that morning, the world had been an ordered and predictable place to Stephen Williamson. Comprehensible. He couldn't go to school; he went instead to the brook at the edge of Beeker Park, skipped stones, climbed a tree whose heaviest branch swung over the brook and thought about Crazy Andrew. It was his first touch with chaos; he was drawn to it and afraid; as he grew older, he was conscious of the possibilities for such chaos in human nature, in himself. Certainly Crazy Andrew had something to do with the order he had searched for in the ministry, in psychology. Certainly he had something to do with the cold spine and nausea he felt in seeing Emily tonight.

He knew the signs.

Chapter Eleven

EMILY KNEW Stephen would go back to his apartment at Thirteenth and Delancey Monday morning. His small suitcase was in the hall.

"You gave me no warning," she said, sitting on the couch, still in her nightgown. ("Mama, I've never seen you in your nightgown at breakfast," Pia had said. "Are you sick?" Emily shook her head, her eyes wet. "You are sick," Pia said decisively. She had never seen her mother cry.)

"I decided this morning," Stephen said. "I have to give these papers in Chicago this week and all my research is at home." He smiled. "I can't work late at night with you here."

"You've known that for weeks," Emily said. "You won't be back."

"Of course I will. I've left my clothes."

"It's because of what you saw me do last night."

Stephen kissed her on the head, went into the hall. Emily followed him.

"What about Pia?" she asked desperately. "You know I have to go back to New York today and you said you'd stay with her."

"We talked about that, Emily," Stephen said with infinite patience. "Pia's coming to my apartment after school today until you get back." He took her face in his hands. "This is for two weeks, Emily," he said. "In two weeks, I'll be in Chicago and back." He squeezed her hand.

"That's very facile and patronizing," she said in a thin dry voice. "Squeezing my hand." And then she lifted the hand he'd squeezed and slapped him with it.

"Emily." He was astonished.

"Go on," she said; her voice was flat. She opened the front door for him.

He had walked past the Clays', three houses up from Emily's, when he heard the slap of her bare feet on the brick pavement behind him. She was running after him still in her nightgown.

"Don't go yet," she said, catching up. "I'm so sorry." He put his coat around her shoulders, his arm around her and walked back to the house with her. Inside the house, he sat down on the couch, pulled her gently down beside him.

"This is not like you to be so frantic."

"I am not like myself," she said quietly. "Things matter more since I fell in love with you." She put her head back against the couch. "Dumb things like seeing my grandfather and what happened to Pia last night. I could've been very academic about these things a year ago. D'you think I'm all right?"

"Yes." He was hesitant.

"You think something."

"I was bothered by last night," he confessed. "I've probably made too much of it. I see so many people who are in trouble."

"No courage." She flopped against his shoulder. "I wish you were a dogcatcher or telephone linesman or something simple."

"I would like that," he said, leaving her calmly this time. "I will give dog-catching some thought while you're in New York."

Emily stood in the middle of the studio, still in her nightgown, sorting through forms of dancers she had sketched through the years, taking out one particular dancer she had drawn the spring before she went to college. The wire-mesh form she had attacked in the midst of a raging headache the night before was flat; she began to bend it back into shape, pulling and straightening the wires to follow the torso line of the dancer she had selected to sculpt, working slowly now, with great deliberation and concentration against the pain in the center of her brain, beginning to grow in short radial circles as though she could feel the point of the protractor spinning the circles larger and larger filling her brain.

Emily had had a friend in grammar school before she was expelled from Friends, Adrienne Sims, a pleasant round mushroom of a girl, and she had loved her passionately, as some children will. For a short time, until Adrienne narrowly escaped, every moment was spent with Adrienne or thoughts of her. Then, one day, Adrienne had brought another friend over to play, a horrible black-haired girl who smelled of sweet perfume, and Emily had thrown a rage, heaved her grandmother's Victorian china dog at Adrienne, cutting her head and causing her to abandon Emily for good. It destroyed the china dog as well and occasioned the one long talk her mother had ever had with her, brought on, she suspected, by the china dog rather than Adrienne Sims's split head, but Emily nonetheless remembered this talk, because she had frightened herself at the power of her own feelings.

"We do not possess other people," her mother had said. "They don't belong to us."

She had raced upstairs in a fury then, locked her door against invasion and taken all her dolls, what had seemed at the time to be hundreds of beautiful Mme. Alexander dolls in finely made dresses given her by her Philadelphia grandmother at every occasion. She had stripped them naked, cut off their hair, slashed their stomachs with bold red paint and danced over their still plaster bodies spread around the floor. Afterwards she had fallen into a dead sleep.

When she awoke much later to the loud pounding of Cinderella on her bedroom door, she was horrified at the limits she had broken.

She spent the night with the door locked pasting the nylon hair back on the violated dolls, washing their bloodied bellies, dressed them back in their finery with hushed words of apology and guilt.

When the morning light came through her bedroom window the next day, it looked as though nothing had happened. But Emily could see the white glue hardened on her doll's heads, and she knew she had seen a darkness in her own soul.

When Emily got on the 10:20 train to New York, the headache had consumed her. Occasionally the spinning world of nothern Jersey outside the windows would be obliterated by a vision of Jane Fielding strung mid-sky from a bathrobe tie, just the head of her, and during the hour-and-a-half trip to Penn Station, Emily became accustomed to erasing the vision, filling the space in front of her with a single color, spilling black paint over northern Jersey. She should not have gone to the Fowlers' yesterday, should not have left Pia with the Burroughses, she thought to herself, but mostly she was busy with the vision of Jane Fielding, which was not content to remain black for very long.

Noontime at Palio's on Forty-second, Emily had wine with lunch; she had the wine but the pain in her head was too fierce to eat. Once, at noon, she had called Stephen. His office line was busy. She called four times in succession and then sat back down. She would wait until one. Andy Brown stayed with her until one. He ate her sandwich and she drank his wine.

"I didn't think you drank, Emily."

"I don't," she said. "Not often." The pain in her head was duller; she was disassembled.

He got up to leave at one.

"You'll be there on time, won't you?" he asked.

"I have always been there on time," she said thickly. "I want to make a phone call first."

Andy came right back, sat down next to her.

"I've always thought you were the rock of Gibraltar, Em, the only reasonable person on the show," he said. "What's wrong?"

"I have a headache," she replied. "A bad one." Her head tumbled when she got up to make a telephone call; she knew she was very drunk, would likely be sick.

In the ladies' room, she lay on the cold tile. One lady came in; she watched her feet under the doors. An attendant came in, called her by name.

"I'm here," Emily said, pulled herself up, washed her face in the sink.

"Man out there says you're to be at the studio. You're half an hour late."

"What time is it?"

"Two-thirty."

"Lord." Emily sat down on a chair next to the telephone. "Tell him I have to make a phone call."

"He's with a patient," Stephen's nurse said.

"It's important."

"Are you a patient?"

"I'm Emily."

"Well . . ." She was indecisive.

"Tell him it's an emergency. Laura Rand has fallen apart."

There was silence. The nurse's voice again. "He wants to call you on another line. What's your number there?"

Emily read off the number on the telephone to the nurse.

"Laura Rand." Stephen's voice clear and warm.

"Stephen." Her throat tightened. "Something's wrong."

"What's wrong?"

"I have a terrible headache."

"It will pass, Emily. Take something for it. Come here when you finish tonight."

"You don't understand," she said, and now the drink was out of her head, the pain was coming back in the vacated space. "It's not an ordinary headache."

"Emily," Stephen said, mildly exasperated. "I can't do anything."

"I know."

"Aren't you supposed to be at the studio?"

"Yes."

"Take something stronger than aspirin, Em. A drink, maybe."

"I did." Her eyes burned. "I will." She hung up.

"You act like we've got all day, Laura." Bilbo stormed in the dressing room.

Agnes finished Emily's make-up.

"I've been working on this scene since seven this morning," he said. "Don't do the lips like that, Agnes, for God's sake. And you blow in drunk at two-thirty."

"Laura's not drunk," Agnes protested.

"Well, she's not sober either." He followed her into the studio. "Lie on the couch."

Emily rested against the couch arm.

"Relax. You know, languid. A come-on. Andy comes in. He's gonna make you. You want him to make you." He clapped his hands over his eyes. "You look more like you're holding on to a roller coaster. Be provocative, for Chrissake."

"Do you feel really bad?" Andy asked. "You want to cut it for today?"

"That's okay," Emily said. "I'll be provocative."

"Okay. Let's go. You guys ready?" he asked the camera crew.

"So you see, Laura," Andy began. "I'm a lonely man. I gave my life for this woman and she wasn't worth my little finger."

There was a long silence.

"Goddammit," Bilbo muttered.

"I forgot," Emily said. "I remember now, but I forgot before."

"Laura Rand remembers. That's just wonderful. Let's try again."

"So you see, Laura," Andy began again. "I'm a lonely man. I gave my life for this woman and she wasn't worth my little finger."

"I know, Andy. We've both had bad luck."

"If only I'd had sense enough to fall for someone like you, Laura." He sat down on the edge of the couch. "Someone sweet, simple, loyal." His hand on her knee.

"I guess I've always liked you, Andy, since we were children."

"You're a lovely thing to look at." Andy moved his hand up to Laura's waist, faced her. "Has anybody ever told you that?"

"Andy." Laura's face strained in concern. "You're not leading me on, are you? To show up Prudence or anything."

"Of course not, Laura," Andy said, kissing her. "I've just found a diamond where I had an ordinary stone."

Silence.

"Line!"

The pain in Emily's head was blinding. She sat up on the couch, pitched over.

Emily lay on a bed in the dressing room. Light-headed.

"The doctor said it was nerves," Andy said, washing off his make-up. "I never thought you had a nerve in your body. Cool as a cucumber." He stretched, leaned back in his chair. "Funny thing. You never know about other people."

"What doctor?"

"Bilbo called a doctor. You didn't know?"

"Vaguely."

"He gave you a shot to relax you." Andy dried his face. "You couldn't feel it?"

"I guess. A little."

"It's supposed to make your head swim."

"It's swimming."

"Headache gone?"

"Yes." Emily rolled on her side. "D'you know Cinderella?"

"Can't say as I do."

"Not the real one."

"Not either one."

"This lady named Cinderella took care of me when I was growing up," Emily said. "Sort of raised me."

"Southern belle, huh. Had a mammy. You hardly seem the type."

"Not exactly."

Emily had dreamed of Cinderella—a long, simple dream of Cindy not as Emily had known her but as Jillian must have known her—Cinderella rocking her, holding her in those long, powerful arms, singing low in her throat out of some distant comfortable memory and waking, softly waking, still in a drug sleep, without any clear distinctions between sleeping and waking. Emily wanted to go back to Cinderella. Back home.

"You okay?" Agnes asked.

"I think," Emily said, straightening her dress, brushing her hair. "I still feel funny. Is Bilbo mad at me?"

"He's not real happy."

"It's good for his ulcer."

"You going home now?"

"Yes." Emily had made up her mind. "I am going home."

I I

PIA MISSED two buses at Thirtieth and Pine because of the fight and by the time the 6:10 L19 came down Pine, it was getting dark and would be dark by the time she got to Stephen's. Gunther still stood against the schoolyard wall, square as a caboose, the blood now caked brick-red and dry on his forehead, on his nose.

"I've got to take this bus," she said apologetically.

"S'all right," he replied, his husky voice thick German. "Take the bus."

The last she saw of him as the cars crowded behind the bus and blocked her view, he was standing clenched and immobile by the schoolyard; she wondered if she would see him again.

It had all started that morning during fifth-grade snack on the playground, Gunther's second day at Friends Select, his fourth day in the United States. The class did not like Gunther from the start; Pia could feel it and even Miss Eleanore Starr, the homeroom teacher (who generally did not feel anything at all except hunger pains during math class and anger most of the time), could feel it and called Pia to her desk after class was dismissed on Gunther's first day. Pia had a reputation for kindness, always, since nursery school, she could be counted on to stand by the outcast, to befriend the child no one liked, in spite of the damage it might do to her reputation. (Fact was, it never damaged her reputation, and even though Friends wrote consistently on her report that she did not live up to her academic potential, and if she didn't read something other than comics and learn fractions, she would have to stay back in fifth grade, everyone had to admit that Pia Fielding was more kind and gentle than most of the children at this urban Quaker school and could be counted on.) Miss Eleanore Starr told Pia to be helpful to Gunther the next day, that there was bound to be trouble.

"Why don't some of the children like him?"

"Because he's German," Miss Starr replied in a tone that suggested the question did not bear answering.

"What's wrong with being German?" Pia persisted. Miss Starr sighed, a long heavy sigh, and rustled the papers on her desk indicating she had said all that she intended to say.

So the next day Pia sat next to Gunther in Meeting and helped him in grammar and shared her music book with him during singing and gave him both her crackers during snack. After recess, there was a swastika on his desk.

"Were you a Nazi?" Pia asked, confused.

"Of course I wasn't. I wasn't even born," he said fiercely. "I am a German."

And later, when Pia opened her reading book, there was a scratch paper written in red ink, "Jew hater."

"What's going on?" she asked Kevin, who was usually one of her close friends.

"I dunno," he said. "No one likes him. Arlie started

it. His father fought against the Germans in the war. He's pretty old."

"Do you like him?"

"Of course not." And then, for good measure, "I hate him."

"But you don't even know him." Pia protested.

"I would hate him if I knew him, I can tell," Kevin said, and in secret he whispered, "There's gonna be a fight after school." Then he threw her an evil glance, "*Jew hater*," and that was the last Pia heard about it until she walked out into the schoolyard on the north side, where no one usually walked, and just outside the walls, five boys in her class, including Kevin and Arlie Dater, who got all excellents and even a triple star in initiative and responsibility, were sitting on the top of the drum belly of Gunther Schultz and beating him bloody.

"Someone's coming!" Arlie shouted as she came around the corner.

"Beat it." And everybody scrambled off Gunther and raced like bandits around the corner. Pia stopped, leaned against the wall and watched Gunther lift himself up slowly, first on his elbow, and then sit spread-legged like a panda bear, blood pouring out of his nose.

"You oughta go to the nurse," Pia said.

"No."

"I'll take you."

"No."

"Are you bad hurt?"

"No."

The first L19 bus came and Pia let it pass.

"That was my bus," she said.

"Then get on it."

"No," she said. "I'll wait with you. They'll be back."

Gunther looked down the street after the boys.

"Yes," he said. "See?"

Pia could see the top of Kevin's head, which was bright red, and Jocko Marlowe's Devils jacket. When the next bus came, twenty minutes later, Gunther asked her to stay.

"Your bus?" he asked.

She nodded.

"There will be another in a short time. Right?"

"I guess," she said. "I've never taken this bus before."

"There'll be another," he said. "You wait." And he looked apprehensively down the street where the boys now stood all in a row against the school wall.

"They won't come back with you here," he said.

They did walk back though, nonchalant, slowly, as if they had days to spare, past Gunther and Pia.

"See ya tomorrow," they said to Gunther.

"Yellow chick," Kevin said to Pia, and they all got on the next bus uptown except Arlie, who went back into school to wait for his mother, who taught science in the upper grades.

So when the next bus came, Pia took it.

Pia told Stephen the story at supper. He made a fancy supper for her first visit to his apartment; there were candles on the table and ice cream.

"You cook better than Mama," Pia said.

"That's not hard to beat," Stephen replied, and they both laughed, for Emily was a very poor cook. "But see how thin she keeps us, which is good for the heart."

Then she told him about Gunther.

"You don't understand, Pia, because you were not

alive, but the Nazis did terrible things to the Jews and it is hard to forgive them." He told her the story of when he was a young boy during the war and poor, without a job, his father without a job, and too old to go off to war, his mother making bandages for the British into the night so her eyes had thick pockets under the pupils from worrying and working. Their grandmother used to give them hope with stories of America, where she had surely never been (had never been out of West End Belfast), how in America the children ate ice cream covered with chocolate on a stick, and the whole idea of that going on in America while we were at war and hungry was so preposterous, so marvelous, that it seemed quite worthwhile to live for.

"But the Jews had no hope. There was no point for them to think of ice cream on sticks."

"Gunther was not even born then."

"Sometimes we pay penalty for what our parents do just because we are the children of such parents."

"That is stupid."

"It is stupid and true." He turned on a record. They cleared the table and did the dishes together. "We have a certain responsibility as children. We have a past, and though we did not make it, it is still part of us," he said. "We can't do away with it. Trouble is, Pia, we are not altogether of our own making."

Pia did her homework on the same desk with Stephen, sitting next to him while he wrote his paper for Chicago.

"Who is Cinderella?" he asked once. "Do you know her?"

"She was Mama's lady who took care of her when

she was growing up. I met her once. Mama used to write to her a lot."

"That's where your mother is. She's gone to Washington to see Cinderella. She called me from New York this afternoon to say she was going and could you stay here until Wednesday."

"How come?"

"She didn't say. She just said she was going and would be back tomorrow night."

Then, tucking Pia in bed that night, Stephen sat in the dark with her for a long time, rubbing her back, twisting her wrists and ankles, like his mother used to do for him, he told her.

"Has Emily had headaches before?" he asked just as Pia was drifting to sleep.

Pia shook her head. "She has never been sick." She turned her head into the pillow. "Never at all."

Stephen did not often think of his family. (In defense. It had been as difficult to leave Belfast as it would have been to remain there.) Sometimes he thought of his mother, multicolored, dashing through the garden to take down the clothes before the rain, raging through the kitchen cursing the wood stove for its slowness, for its burning, for its wood smell, but he seldom thought of his father, or if he did, it was a cold rectangular thought, arranged like a catalogue of moral axioms that organized his father's daily life.

But this evening, sitting in the soft darkness beside the sleeping Pia, he remembered a moment with his father he had not allowed himself to remember before.

Stephen had not been a thoroughly good child surely in his growing up, but he had not been bad either. Not as bad as he would have liked to be—not as the boys whose fathers stopped off for ale at the Headless Woman after they left the factory or made merry with Mrs. Wilkens, who had a house on Drury behind the pub. So when he got to university, he broke out like a bull through a fence, drank ale till he toppled off Woolcoat's bronze horse in nothing but his undershorts, went back to Mrs. Wilkens's three times in one night, finally put out on the streets for rowdiness and told not to come round again until he knew how to behave—then practiced his behavior, nearly sober, on a poor convent girl not yet eighteen, very plump and soft and innocent and scared to her round feet boxed in black oxfords.

"You have no class, Stephen," his old friend Michael told him. "That poor dear Catholic child would eat a pine tree if you told her to."

So Stephen skipped the Irish altogether and took on an American girl from New York City who was in Belfast for a year, or thought he took her, but he was very drunk when they made love, so he was never sure whether he had taken her or not and she was gone when he woke up.

The university told him it was likely he would be at work at the factory himself in a month if he didn't settle down a little more, which he did try to do, but his energy was at a level too grand for scholarship. It was entirely suited to revolution, so he joined the Irish Nationals on campus, spoke in moving poetry (written by his friend Michael) on the university steps, and became in a brief term the first half-Protestant half-Catholic leader of the Irish Nationalist party at the university.

"You draw people like flypaper," Michael had said with admiration. "It's quite extraordinary. You should be a professional revolutionary," he confided, "Except you are hopeless with women."

"I could be a revolutionary until I'm twenty or so, but my family's put out with me," he said, not without some pleasure. "My father won't go to church, so my mum says, because of the shame I've brought to him."

Which was quite true. Adine Williamson had gone to Stephen's flat, something she simply would never do —to tell him that though his father could bear the pain of his carousing and womanizing and falling drunk off horses, it was too much to expect him to accept Stephen's political activity. And she was Catholic too, Catholic and Irish to the marrow of her bones, so Stephen knew it was serious indeed.

It did not stop him surely, but it made what he was doing at the university seem very significant. He was, however, too caught up in the sense of his own spirit to notice the rising tide against the Irish Nationalists on campus, so when there was retaliation and the police were called in and were very harsh with the Irish Nationalist, particularly Stephen, he was stunned.

He was more sober than he'd been in months when his father walked into the police station in work clothes with his black lunch pail, predictably humorless and stiff. Mr. Williamson talked to the officers in a back office; and when he came out, the officer who had brought Stephen in told him he could go now. Stephen kept a pace behind his father, walking home.

"I thought you'd given up on me," he said.

"No," his father replied.

"Mother said you were angry." He was neither arrogant nor contrite.

"I have been angry," he replied.

"You have not given up on me?" Stephen persisted, angling for the commitment he knew was there.

"I am your father," Ronald Williamson had answered. Stephen wanted to reach out to him; he did not dare.

I I I

HER BROTHER CHARLES took Emily. He knew where Cinderella lived because he mailed the checks to her every week.

"I decided to send her weekly checks," he said magnanimously, "so that she didn't spend everything that Dad left here at once."

"Cinderella wouldn't," Emily replied. "She is smarter than most of us. Possibly even you." Charles was in his last year at Harvard, home for special research on the Hill. Margaret too was in college and Jillian, eleven now, living in Washington at the same house with a housekeeper.

They pulled up to the row house at Thirteenth and Q—lines of row houses, once elegant when the city of Washington bustled by the Capitol and Cleveland Park, where Emily had grown up, was just a summer outpost for wealthy families. The houses on Q Street were barred now, three stories up, with double locks on the doors, or vacant with broken windows, or for sale. People clustered in threes on street corners, swinging on an iron gate or sitting folded from drink or dope on porches.

"I'll stay in the car," Charles said, rolled up his side window, locked the door.

Emily got out. Her headache had subsided in anticipation; she was light-headed.

A very old man in an undershirt without the sleeves answered the door. The house behind him was dark. He squinted in the porch light.

"Is Cinderella Diggs here?" Emily asked.

"Cinderella?" He turned around and called behind him, "Irmy, where'd Cinderella get to?" And then, back facing Emily, "Who are you, child?"

"I'm Emily Fielding," she said.

"Never heard of you."

"Cinderella raised me."

"Never heard of you."

Emily started. "Are you Cinderella's father?"

The old man cackled then. "Cinderella's father? You hear that Irmy?" Irmy came up. She was younger, not young, but of undetermined age, in a large flowered dress, pinned together at the front, and bright red material wound around her head. "Cinderella ain't no child of mine."

"You get on back in your chair now, Papa." Irmy said. "What you want with Cinderella?"

Emily was beginning to perspire, hot and cold, under the skin. "She's a friend of mine. I want to see her."

"She's not here."

"When will she be back?"

"She's not coming back." The woman came out on the porch with Emily. "What's the matter with you, child, shaking like you are?"

"I guess I'm cold." Emily pulled her light trenchcoat around her. "I'm Emily Fielding," she said.
"Cinderella raised me."

"Oh, yes." The woman's frown faded. "Cinderella's
told me about you." The woman stood back. "Go on in
the house." Emily walked in the front room, the living
room, which was dark except for a light where the old
man was sitting, reading. A man or a woman, it was too
dark to tell, was sleeping on the couch, snorting in
short breaths.

"Remember that child Cinderella told us about,
Papa?"

The old man nodded.

"This is her."

"I knew that, Irmy—if only you weren't so bossy, I'd
have told you."

"Cinderella's clean forgotten in this house," the body
on the couch, which turned out to be the body of a man,
said. He stopped snoring, spoke clear as cymbals. "Same
as if she was dead."

Emily followed Irmy to the back of the house to a
little room off the kitchen. "This was Cinderella's
room," she said. "We're fixing it up now for my cousin."
She went over to the bureau and opened a drawer.
"Cinderella's my cousin too, and that no-count man in
there, sleeping his life away on the couch, was her
husband come back four months ago after being gone
for fifteen years and now plum mad at Cinderella for
going off."

She brought a picture out of the bureau in a cheap
tin five-and-ten-cent-store frame and gave it to Emily—
a picture of Emily when she was about ten, scowling in
blue jeans, and Cinderella, her long arms wrapped

around Emily's shoulders, she could feel them now, and on her face the look of a woman who knows more than she might want to know, not bitter, but surely wise, perhaps resigned.

"You can keep it," the woman Irmy said. "Cinderella didn't like a lot of folks, but she liked you. She talked about you as if you were her own flesh and blood."

Emily pushed the picture into her pocket.

"Where's she gone?" Emily asked again.

"Chicago."

"For what?"

"For who knows what? The woman raised her arms to the ceiling. "Two months ago, maybe more, Cinderella met this no-good white man. No good." She drew it out. "And Cindy wasn't anybody's fool. She knew he was no good, so I don't know what got into her."

"She went off with him?"

"Last week he said he had to leave for Chicago and parts west. She packed her bags, quit her job and went off to Chicago with him the next day."

Charles had been smoking with the windows shut. Emily got in the car next to him and closed her eyes against the growing pain in her head. The smoke was too dense to breathe.

"Cinderella's gone," she said.

Charles shrugged, turned on the engine and drove off down Q Street.

Chapter Twelve

THE PLANE was high and leveling over the city, gray-blue in early November, a distant slate world spread out beneath them. They dipped forward, rocked and turned east to Philadelphia. The stewardess spilled coffee on the seat beside him, and the woman sitting there moved away, so Stephen had the seats to himself—three abreast, squared in by the high-back chairs, only a small space of light beside him to connect him with the disappearing world of Chicago.

He unfastened his seat belt, lit a cigarette and took the letter Emily had given him to read when he left Philadelphia two weeks ago. It was dated July, this year, right after he had met her: "To the Fielding Children: Dear Margaret, Charles and Jillian," it began.

Stephen and Emily had gone to Alfio's around the corner from his apartment the night she'd gotten back from losing Cinderella in Washington.

"What do you mean, you lost her?" he had asked as they settled themselves in the booth at the very back of the restaurant, where the general rowdiness of the front room would not disturb them.

"Just that," Emily said. "She had gone off with a man."

"Not so surprising."

"You didn't know Cinderella," she said.

There was something all wrong about Emily this evening, as though her clothes had not been sewn together at the seams. She had on a long, thin dress, too cool for autumn, and her hands were dirty.

"Paint?" he asked, taking her fingers in his own.

"Blood," she said matter-of-factly.

"Blood?" He looked at her hands more carefully under the dim candlelight. It was blood and dirt. Her hands were skinned. "What happened?"

"I fell on the way to meet you," she said. "On Pine. I had to run to catch the bus."

"You should wash them, Emily."

"I was afraid you wouldn't be here when I came."

"Where would I go?" He got up, helped her up. "Go wash them now."

"What is it, Emily?" he asked her when she came back.

"It's nothing," she replied vacantly. "I just thought you might leave." She brushed her hair, fallen predictably over her face. "Stephen," she said. "I have changed my mind." She leaned forward to look at him, although her eyes were unconnecting. "I do want to marry."

"You do?"

"I decided in Washington," she said. "Just on the train coming up." She tried to laugh. "It seemed very silly of me not to want to marry, I thought to myself, just because my parents had a bad marriage. It seemed very silly to worry about their marriage."

She knew before she told him that Stephen had retreated: she felt like a child scrambling to get him.

"You have changed your mind?"

Their dinner came. She pushed her plate away, drank

her wine, poured a second glass from the ruby carafe.

"What has come over you?"

"I have headaches," she said without explanation. "You would like out." Her voice was steel-edged.

"Eat something."

"You can't simply send me home with a prescription for getting better, can you?" She threw her head back, assumed a fatherly voice. "Now, dearie, run on home and take two Bufferin, no more, think pleasant thoughts about your childhood and do a good turn for someone. Thirty dollars. I'll see you next Tuesday, same time. Pretty dress, dearie. It becomes you. Always wear lavender and do your hair."

"Hush, Emily."

"You haven't the courage for a relationship with anyone but a patient who is perfectly safe and under your control." She was shaken. She got up and left the restaurant.

When Stephen caught up with her after paying the bill, she was leaning against a streetlight post.

"Emily?"

"Never mind," she said. "Let's just go home."

"Are you going to your own apartment?" she asked Stephen when they got back to Emily's house in West Philadelphia.

"I was planning to stay here."

"I'm glad," she said. She pulled the shades in the bedroom they had shared. Undressed.

But Stephen could not make love.

When Emily finally fell asleep, a troubled, restless sleep, he went downstairs and slept on the couch.

The next morning, before he left for Chicago, Emily gave him the letter to read while he was away. It was for her a desperate move.

He folded the letter in squares with great care and put it in his coat breast pocket; his hands were stone cold; he could not swallow. Surely he had failed Emily. He didn't have the courage for a relationship, as she had said.

He remembered one evening along the quay, along the Irish Sea—the Sea churning at their feet, headstrong and unrelenting like the Irish. Margaret, barely pregnant, and Stephen (it must have been the last time, or near to last, he felt invincible, full to laughter of his enormous possibilities) danced the quay together. Dusk, all the sensible people gone in for tea, to brace themselves against the coming cold. They danced the length of it, stopped in the market for tiny shrimp in bags. Margaret fed him with her round hands, making music in her throat like a bird. He leaned on the pier post, her warm body against him, against the wind whisking off the sea and ate the sweet shrimp she fed him.

"D'you suppose we will go on and on like this?" she'd asked.

"Surely we will," he had replied bravely. "Only better."

"Sometimes," she started, grown melancholy as she was wont to do when they'd been gay. "Oh, never mind."

"Don't be foolish and worry yourself old for nothing." He'd swung her in his arms around the pier post. "We are young, Margaret Williamson, we are young. We don't need to live in the shadows." He kissed her bright red hair, thick and soft as silk thread. "We can live in the morning sun."

He had let himself fall in love with Emily Fielding at a time when she had seemed to him as invincible as Stephen dancing on the quay. He ought to have known better. He didn't have the courage for this woman who had born witness, as he had just read, to such failure of blood. Surely her excellent fiber was strained now, had weakened beyond repair. He felt himself take hold as he had done when he had first left Ireland, pull in like a wet soft-bodied snail pulls in, under the hard shell. Inviolate. Instinctively he knew Emily would not recover.

V

Emily Alone

Chapter Thirteen

EMILY'S HEADACHES were worse. They attacked without mercy, sometimes in the middle of the night. Black vengeance without reprieve. Stephen had been gone two weeks.

"Maybe you'll get well when Stephen comes home," Pia said hopefully. She had gone to school those two weeks because she had to, but the rest of the time she stayed with Emily in the studio.

Emily was working on the form of a dancer. It was a new dancer, more complete than anything she had done—free-form, concentric circles. Unrestrained.

"Maybe," Emily said. She had gone to see Dr. Amos Little (the first time she had visited a psychiatrist on business), who had given her a green-and-brown capsule every eight hours and no more, but it only worked for two hours, if that. She didn't go back to Amos Little; she knew he wanted to talk to her, to find out what was going on, and she didn't want to talk at all. Never had. She wanted charge of her own life without such conditions.

The first week Stephen was gone Emily left "Better Promises." She had gone to New York to film the last of the series she had failed to film the week before when she'd been ill. It went very well at first, but her face quivered in the close-ups.

"Christ," Bilbo had shouted.

"I can't help it," Emily had said.

"You can't help it," he'd muttered.

She had left the stage, the studio, gone upstairs to the producer's office and left the show.

"You can't," Al Caparni said. "We'll wait. Two months, three months, y'know. Take your time. You'll get better."

"I have to leave now, Al," Emily said quietly.

"Impossible. Plain impossible. We've got the next two months written and you figure big. One really juicy love affair. You'll love it." He grabbed her hand, gave it a big kiss. "Come on, Emily." Al Caparni had known her since she was nineteen, had hired her initially. He was a tough professional man with few weaknesses, but Emily was one of them.

"Get someone," Emily said. "It shouldn't be hard."

"Oh, sure. Get someone else. Y'know what those round bellies in Jersey'd do if I got another Laura Rand? Boycott the show!"

"Al, please."

He shook his head, unbelieving. "You're serious," he said.

"I am."

"You're really serious." He rested his head in his hands. "We'll simply have to kill Laura then," he said brashly, intending to hurt her.

Emily shrugged. "Kill her."

"Okay, we'll do that." His voice rose. "After ten years, it really doesn't matter to you." He got up, moved his chair over closer to Emily. "Just kill her, the lady says."

"If you're not going to get a replacement."

He began again. "How about six months off? Laura can have an accident. Go to Europe."

"I am leaving, Al." She had made up her mind.

He was crying when he walked her down Forty-second to find a taxi—a cool and crafty man with a reputation for meanness.

"You didn't even give us a chance to give you a party," he said. "Or a watch. Y'know, the junk people give."

"I wanted to slip out quietly."

"If you change your mind. Like even next year. We'll wait. We won't do anything drastic."

At the last minute, he got in the cab with her and went to Pennsylvania Station, walked her all the way to the five o'clock fast train to Philadelphia and Washington.

"Emily, you look so bad."

"I have headaches," she said.

He ruffled her hair, held her back from getting on the train until the last minute.

"You'll be okay?" It was a question.

Emily nodded.

"You won't crap around now, Laura Rand, will you?" he asked, not ready to let her go. "You'll take care of yourself."

"Thank you, Al."

He stood on the platform until the train had gone.

Lately Emily had nightmares. Waking nightmares working in her studio and nightmares that woke her at dawn so she could not go back to sleep.

Once she was Martin Fielding an April morning in 1956, ten years before, wound tight to springing by the frustration of the years.

"Jane."

"Martin. What are you doing here at this house? I have my dance class."

"About the children."

"Honestly, Martin." A raw laugh, harsh as oyster shells. "This is foolish, isn't it?" Foolish. Inept and impotent. She has diminished you to a slender pinprick on the surface of her skin. "You have your practice to attend to. Surely you cannot handle the children."

"Better me than you," he shouts, and in a language he does not know how to use: "Whore."

She rises taller than the room, her head passes through the ceiling, up through the roof. Her body thin and white as celery, wrapped loosely in a blue silk robe. She shakes her thick black hair in the morning sun.

"Who wouldn't be a whore with such a man?"

The blue sash hangs like an arm in satisfaction across her hipbone, her slender thigh daring his impertinence; the wire wound tight in his brain splits, spins off, unravels with electric sparks. He grabs the blue sash and rips it from her waist. The robe falls open, her skin is milk-white against the dense black forest, open to invasion. He would rape her clean to the cool dark center of her eyeballs.

"Martin." Shrill. Perhaps afraid.

He knocks her to the ground. For all her power, she is frail at the end.

She is too proud to speak again. She knows her victor, fights vainly with her arms. He fastens them down with his knees, whips the sash around her neck and pulls with the sure white hands of a surgeon, hands always clean in the ancient cracks of age. He pulls only as long as necessary and then gets up. It was perhaps too easy in the end. He does not look down, takes instead the dining room rug, just six feet wide, and wraps her beautiful still body into the center of it.

This time, sleeping, she is her mother, Jane Fielding.

"Martin." She sits in the dining room, drinking her coffee, and rises to meet him in the hall. He is red-faced, absurd, blustering like a carrot-headed boy against his own inadequacy.

"What in God's name are you doing here this time of the morning, Martin?"

"I came about the children."

"Again?" She is exasperated. She has possessed this man, subdued him easily without recourse to tricks and possessed him full. He has been small compensation. "We have been through this before and before and before."

He is angry this time. His florid face shakes and reddens, bright as Jell-O.

Emily's hair is wet with perspiration; her hands and feet are cold.

"Mama," Pia cried. Emily grappled with the light, sat up. Pia was spread across her. "Lord," she said, shaking the last scene out of her head.

"I've been trying to wake you, Mama."

"How come?"

Pia curled in the corner of the bed now, wrapped together like a stricken cat.

"My stomach hurts," she said. "Just awful."

Her head was cold and wet.

Emily got up, dressed automatically.

"Is something going to happen?"

"I don't know, Pia." Emily controlled her voice, sliding between two worlds, the residue of her mother's dream still clinging to the edge of consciousness. She bent over Pia, lying her on her back, pressed her hand in the place along the right side of her stomach she remembered her own father pressing.

"Does it hurt there?" she asked.

"It hurts all over," Pia said. "Is it something?"

"It could be an appendicitis." Emily lifted Pia, wrapped her in a blanket, carried her downstairs.

"You think something's going to happen, don't you?" Pia asked, pressing her head into the warmth of her mother's shoulders.

"I think you might have an appendicitis," Emily said softly. "If that's true, what will happen is the doctors will take out your appendix."

"That's all."

Emily put Pia in the back of the car. Pine Street was empty, a damp, cold night, pale circles around the streetlights, smoke circles like moons in front of them.

"That's all."

A man in a street fight was brought into the next room in the Emergency corridor. He hollered obscenities about his mother and brother, and the resident who had started to look at Pia was called out with the street fighter; he was gone a long time.

Emily stood by the bed in the middle of the starched green room.

"I think it's getting better," Pia said. "D'you think we should leave?"

"We should find out what it is."

"What if it's nothing?"

"Then we go home."

Pia held her mother's hand. "Do you have a head-ache?"

"A little." And conscious of Pia's concern, "Not much."

The resident, who was from India, small and gentle, said it was not appendicitis. He took Emily outside into the corridor.

"It is not anything at all that I can see," he said, and quietly, so Pia could not hear him, "Has she had troubles? I have known troubles to give a terrible pain in the stomach."

"You don't think she should stay overnight?"

"There is no reason." The man in the next room shouted for the doctor; the nurse motioned to him from the door. "This is a dreadful place for spending the night."

The gentle Indian doctor stuck his head in the car just as Emily was about to pull out of the emergency room parking lot.

"Where do you live?"

"Down Pine," she replied. "About ten blocks."

"I come." He climbed in the front seat next to Pia. "The other resident replaces me now, and it is no place for a woman and child here where there are street fights in the middle of the night."

The doctor carried Pia upstairs and put her down on Emily's bed. She was very nearly his size.

"There," he said. "You have a good sleep and tomorrow your bellyache will be gone." He pulled the covers
up to her chin. "But your troubles will still be there.
You say to them then: troubles, you are like the wind
and I can outrun you."

"Would you like something to drink? Coffee or
wine?" Emily asked. "I have very little in the house
today."

"Nothing," he replied.

"You won't sit down?"

"Oh, no." He pulled up his coat collar against the
night cold. "I have only come to keep you from street
fights," he said, "and I am touched by you alone with
this child." He smiled and left on foot walking down
Pine Street back to the hospital residences. Emily was
touched as well. No one had ever come home with her
simply to keep her from street fights.

She leaned against the bedroom wall and watched her
daughter. The lines of living—even children have them
around the eyes and mouth—sink in sleep. The skin,
sacklike, encases them like seeds to germinate in sun-
light. If troubles caused that bellyache, then surely the
belly would burst before the troubles sorted out.

Emily knew her power. She had a firm hold on the
process of living, the day-to-day getting by without losing ground (even with the pain in her head, her
mother's corpse unearthed, she had survived). But something new had happened. She had raised from birth a
daughter linear, a child to love and sustain, to teach

the rudimentry forms of physical survival, and now this child had doubled in upon herself, grown complex, multilayered, and the process of living was not enough to sustain her any longer. It was no good a mother fighting madness like an angry Spartan in the night.

In the cool rational part of her brain, a slender corner that remained pure in the worst hours of her night, Emily took control.

Pia's arm rested comfortably outside the sheet; she took her hand.

Emily went to the offices of Harper and Harper at Twelfth and Chestnut after she took Pia to school the next morning—they were worn ebony with deep leather chairs as cracked and wrinkled with age as Mr. Harper, who was the son of the first Harper and only came in on Wednesdays to see old clients or their children. They were offices that had the dullness and quiet dignity of the Philadelphia lawyers who had grown old in them, and Emily came now because Mr. Harper was the family lawyer, Henry Fowler's classmate, Lydia's cousin. He was glad to see Emily; he wanted to hear the details of how Lydia's death had affected Henry, since no one at church seemed to know and the battalion of nurses at Tredifferin wouldn't let anyone near Henry. Besides, he was curious about Emily. He thought she lived preposterously, but he had enough life in him to be curious about her.

She wrote out the paper she wanted to have him sign in longhand on Harper and Harper stationery. He read it, signed it, got his aged secretary to sign it, and only as he walked her to the door did he think to ask her who was this Stephen Williamson.

"A friend," she answered.

"Another friend?" he asked with just a hint of dis-approval. "You have still never married?"

She smiled; he asked her that always.

"And never will." He answered it himself. "All right, Emily. You take care."

The morning sun was too bright for November; and already this day her head had begun its ravage.

Mrs. Levy was standing on the corner of Fortieth and Pine when Emily got off the bus, talking to Mrs. Ernie Lustig, who lived next door, and Aunt Sadie from round the corner and Bill Something who was a student and rented a room from Mrs. Levy on the third floor. Emily almost went by the stop when she saw them there, but they had seen her standing at the door and waved, anxious to tell her something.

"So, we hear you quit the show." Mrs. Levy couldn't wait for her to get off the bus.

"Yes," Emily replied. "Last week."

"Have you seen it this week?" Aunt Sadie asked.

Emily shook her head.

"You never watch yourself?" Bill was impressed.

"Sometimes." Emily tried to walk on. "Lately I've been busy."

"Well, it didn't say you quit. It said you were on leave, and then just yesterday they mentioned—it was Andy Brown, I think—said Laura Rand'd been in an accident in Spain or somewhere."

"It's permanent," Emily said. "My leave from the show is permanent."

"D'ya hear the fight last night?" Bill asked. "Right

here on this corner. We were talking about it when you came up.''

"This used to be a perfectly respectable neighborhood and now street fights every night," Mrs. Levy said. "I raised my children here with no trouble."

"There was a young man," Aunt Sadie began.

"A man, y'a hear, Bill?"

Bill had heard.

"You don't even have to be a woman to be beat up any longer. Doesn't help a bit to be a man."

"Three teen-agers beat a young man right on this corner about one o'clock last night." Mrs. Levy couldn't wait for Aunt Sadie.

"I heard it," Aunt Sadie said proudly.

"You're always hearing things, Sadie," Mrs. Ernie Lustig said. "He was from India or Pakistan—one of those places. I think he was a doctor. That's what the police said."

"You're sure he wasn't Japanese? There's one lives down the way."

"An Indian doctor from the hospital. The police ought to know the difference between an Indian and a Jap, now don't you think?"

Emily started. "Was he badly hurt?" Her throat shrank closed.

"Well," Aunt Sadie began.

"Not bad, Sadie," Mrs. Ernie Lustig said. "The police told me he wasn't bad hurt."

"But he was hurt, Mrs. Lustig," Mrs. Levy said. "It's the principle of the thing. Of not being able to stand on your own street corner."

"But in the middle of the night. Who's gonna be

standing on his own street corner at one in the morning,
I ask you?"

They did not even notice that Emily had left. She
went in the house, into the living room, and lay down
on the couch. She seemed to still hear Mrs. Levy, but all
the windows were closed.

Andy Brown and Prudence were in the kitchen when
Emily turned on the television.

"So you think Laura's going to have to stay in the
hospital in Spain?"

"For a long time, as I hear it from her mother."

"Laura Rand has the worst luck."

Prudence sat down at the kitchen table. "You know,
Andy, I thought you were interested in her for a while."

"Me?" Andy sat down, took Prudence's hand. "Not
me, Prudence. Laura's a nice girl and I hope she's going
to be all right, but I've never been interested in anyone
but you."

I I

THE DANCER WAS DONE. In the early dusk from the
studio skylight a sultry November, the circles of her
body, silver with their own life, seemed to take flight.
Emily ran her hand over the curve line of her back, a
slender half-moon. She knew it was a splendid dancer.

On the radio, Mussorgsky. Emily began to dance,
slowly, as she might have done when she was a child,
and unselfconsciously testing the possibilities of her own
body—but she had never danced, had always been too

tall and awkward, although she had felt the need to dance contained just beneath her skin; the urgency within take form, spinning magnificently, dropping her conscious body behind her like a gown. Jane Fielding had been the dancer. But Emily was dancing now, bending, whirling through the studio with such a sense of power and release, the world inside the studio cracked into a kaleidoscope of colors as she swung around the center of the room.

"Mama."

Emily stopped short. Breathless.

"What are you doing?" Pia accused.

"Dancing." Emily laughed, awkward at being discovered. She caught herself on the work table.

"Dancing?" Pia asked. "All by yourself?"

"Haven't you ever?" Emily slid down to the floor, sat cross-legged. "I used to dance all by myself when I was your age."

"I never have." Pia looked at her as though she were a stranger.

"Besides, I thought you were at Sally Hawkins's until after supper."

"We had a fight." Pia walked over to the dancer Emily had done. "You're finished."

"I think," Emily said, still uncomfortable with her daughter's unspoken accusation. "I hate to think of anything I've done as finished, though."

"I like her." Pia ran her fingers along the edges of the dancer's abstract face. "She looks like you, kind of."

"Like me?" Emily laughed. "I'm so clumsy."

"In the face, I mean. Just the feeling of you." She sat down next to her mother, put her head in Emily's lap.

"Will Stephen be back day after tomorrow?"

"Possibly," Emily said, "though he thought he might stay in Chicago until Friday." She unbraided Pia's hair, ran her fingers through the waves. "Have you missed him?"

"I have missed him a great deal," Pia said. "You haven't. You've hardly mentioned him since he's been gone."

"I haven't thought of anything since Stephen's been gone," Emily confessed, "because of these stupid headaches."

"Do you have a headache now?"

"I have one all the time."

Pia wrapped her arms around her mother's neck and kissed her forehead.

"I don't know what to do about it," Pia said.

"Me neither," Emily replied, rubbing her head against her daughter's sharp shoulder.

I I I

IT WAS EIGHT IN THE MORNING and Pia had left for school. Emily went out on the screened back porch. It was bright and cold; she had been up all night. From where she stood, she could see the corner where the Indian doctor had been beaten and Mrs. Levy's back porch where she hung her sheets and the bus down Pine Street and the veterinary hospital, reputed to be one of the best in the country, and a mirror against the screen ledge in which Pia had studied her face all summer. Now double, the mirror, the veterinary hospital, Mrs. Levy's white and colored sheets. Emily squinted, to narrow her vision, now in threes and blurred fours. She picked up the mirror from the screen ledge.

The early sun was behind her, so her body made a long, dark shadow against the late-autumn leaves and the figure in the mirror was dark. Not an ordinary darkness either but a golden dark. She looked carefully at the clouded form, first multiple, double, now single. Certainly it was not Emily Fielding that she saw. A face, however, not unfamiliar. In fact, familiar. Strangely so. And as her eyes became accustomed to the light behind her, the glare it made on the glass, the woman in the mirror cleared and with a start, Emily recognized her as Jane Fielding. Her mother. She had gone mad.

She replaced the mirror on the ledge, walked with great care into her bedroom, shutting the porch door behind her, down the corridor and the front steps, through the kitchen and into her studio. Her head beat like a drum inside her brain. She was the moment of percussion in a symphony rising to its definition. Neither desperate nor resigned. The pain in her head was too great.

I V

STEPHEN'S PLANE ARRIVED AT 10:30. He had intended to go straight to his office, but when he got in the taxi, he gave the driver Emily's address, let himself into the house on Pine Street with his own key.

The house was silent.

"Emily." He went to the foot of the stairs and called, "I'm here." There was no answer.

He went through the kitchen.

"Emily?"

The studio door was ajar. Inside the air was smoky, the thick sullen light through the long windows played tricks with shadows, and the simple abstracted form of a woman dancer in the center of the room was broken and repeated in dark patterns that dashed across the floorboards.

"Emily," he called. He had a sense of another presence which told him in a dark way he was not alone.

"Emily." He moved swiftly across the room and threw open the large closet where material and tools were stored. The cool light from the studio rushed by him and he saw her face on, hanging lifeless by a rope from the ceiling.

VI

Stephen and Pia: Easter 1967

Chapter Fourteen

EASTER IN BELFAST. Stephen had brought Pia to Ireland in early April, when the daffodils on the Common had just begun to bloom straight and stiff as British warriors and today, waiting to go to the airport and home, the daffodils were such a mass of splendid color you could not see a single military stalk.

"Lordy, how the color of the daffs will be," his mother had said on their way from the airport three weeks ago.

"Lordy, how the color of the daffs is come," she said today.

The air wet as birth water and clear with a gentle distant sun making this corner of the island a miracle. Such a day as only happens once or twice in a single year to tug at the life source, to make a man rich and tender with living. A sunburst of daffodils at full bloom.

Such was the state of Stephen Williamson standing outside the ordinary house where he'd been born forty years ago, his mind lingering on the edge between this day and other days. Something in the quiet spirit of the moment allowed him to think of Emily again.

Everyone was there to say good-bye. His family, thirty of them at least, counting his Catholic relations and the people from his former parish who'd sent a representa-

tive from the parish and then all come themselves besides and the people in the row houses along the Common.

His mother wore a new dress.

"The first she's bought since you were married,
mind," his sister Eila said.

And an old hat, probably his grandmother's for going
to funerals, dressed to stand outside the cottage and bid
her youngest son good-bye again. The suitcases were
lined up on the streetside for Stephen's brother to take
to the airport. Pia sat on one of them with Mrs.
O'Malley and Aunt Rose; she was munching a scone
with difficulty.

"Now just you try one of my filled scones, dearie,"
Aunt Rose had said after Pia had finished off the plain
scone. "Herbert said they were the best in Belfast, God
rest his soul." So Pia tried Aunt Rose's scone as she had
Aunt Eila's tarts and Sally's shortbreads and Auntie
Terry's sweet-cream pie and sweets and sweets and sweets
until there was a little pouch beneath her belt and she
thought she would probably burst before they got back
to America.

She had laughed in Belfast for the first time in six
months, sitting on the pub stool with General Alphonse
Lafayette, so he called himself, Stephen's Uncle Mac—
drinking ginger beer. She had danced with the foolish
general and laughed at his stories and sung American
songs for the whole crowd who had come to the Headless Woman to see Stephen Williamson come back after
ten years.

"Now, Stephen." His mother pulled him off to sit
with her on the wall outside the cottage. "You cannot
stay away again ten years. It is too long."

"I'll be back more often now," Stephen agreed. "It was hard to come back. Now I've done it, it'll be easier next time."

"And that child, bless my soul, how you'll ever raise a child without a mother, I'll never know."

"I'll manage."

"The parish would have you back *at any time*," she emphasized. "You know that, Stephen."

"Of course I know that, Mother." He hugged the shoulders, aged now and gone to bone. "But I won't be back. You know that."

"You've got to think of your father," she cautioned. "He is getting on and has trouble with his gall bladder, and not to tell your brother when he takes you to the airport, but he had a funny thing in his heart last year and the doctor said 'Mind these funny things with the heart, Ronald,' " his mother reported earnestly. "So you see, it's no good you stay away so long again."

Then she shook her head with the ground-out wisdom of a woman who's raised seven children to her satisfaction with no help.

"You will need to find a mother for this child."

"Not necessarily," Stephen replied. "Emily raised Pia without a father until she died. I can carry on."

He had not always thought he could carry on.

Emily's cleaning lady Sammy, who came on Wednesday every other week, had found Stephen when Emily died. Found him a caged animal gone wild, beating with his fists the finished dancer in the center of the studio floor.

"Mercy," she had whispered, "mercy." But when she

found the body of Emily Fielding, she had wailed so
even Mrs. Levy down the street could hear her and
come up and call the police and Maybel who did day
work for Mrs. Levy and Sammy's husband to come take
Sammy home and finally Dr. Amos Little—all the time,
Stephen out of control, barely subdued by the police,
and then Amos Little beside him on a bed or couch,
muttering, "Jesus Christ."

Once Stephen had gone into the bathroom and
cracked the glass on the medicine cabinet.

"You've got to pull together," Amos said, coming into
the bathroom after Stephen. He ground his hand into
the broken glass until it bled.

"Christ, Stephen, I'm going to have to give you something to knock you out."

"Knock me out, then," Stephen had said. "Do something, for God's sake."

He ripped Emily's bed apart, fell exhausted against
the pillow.

"She even made the bed this morning," he had said.

Amos met Pia when she came home from school. The
Burroughses were there, even Amy and Mrs. Levy, who
never left all day, and Denis Johnson, who lived on the
other side, and Aunt Sadie and the Slocum children,
though the Slocums didn't come, just sent their children.

"It's just awful, just awful," Mrs. Levy said when
Stephen came downstairs some time later to see Pia.
"That poor child."

"Where is she now?"

"Gone to the kitchen," one of the Slocums said.

"Maybe the studio," someone else suggested.

"I think she's sitting on the back porch."

"She didn't want any of us with her," Mrs. Burroughs said, poised for action. "So we had to respect her wishes." And without a breath, "I'll bring over your dinner tonight. I have a casserole in the freezer."

In fact, Pia was gone. Not in the kitchen, in the studio, on the back porch. Stephen slammed the studio door, leaned against it and wept.

Aunt Rose pulled Stephen over to her front yard next door, separated from his own by a high brick wall.

"Now, Stevie, boy, I've some things for you." She tucked two packages in his pocket.

"Scones?"

"Shortbreads. A few for the ride home," she said. "I expect they hardly feed you on these airplanes they have now."

"Rosie, they feed us on the hour. We've been fed so much this month, we'll never eat again."

"Now the other package is for Pia. It's my grand-mother's salts bottle."

"That's very kind of you, Rosie," Stephen said. "She may very well be in need of a salts bottle one day."

"It's the thought, Stevie. You know that. I don't think young people use salts these days."

Stephen straightened the shawl over his aunt's shoul-ders.

"One more thing," she said, businesslike. "I've made my will, Stephen, and I want you to know that the wal-nut bookcase in there is yours and every book in it which my Albert bought—God rest his soul—is for you too, case your brother, Peter, lays a claim on them, him being here when I pass on and you not."

"I'll make sure of that, Rosie."

"And one more thing about your mother, Stevie." She pulled him over, whispered in his ear. "I suppose she hasn't told you about her kidneys."

"Why, no."

"She wouldn't. But the doctor says she may have to have an operation. Now mind she won't tell you and don't say a word of it to her."

"Not a word, Rosie."

"But I think maybe you should get back here more than you do, Stevie. We don't get any younger, y'know."

"You've done well, Rosie. Mother'd be proud of you."

It was getting on till four. His plane left Belfast at eight. He hoped he'd see his father before he left. Ron Williamson at sixty-five still working the seven-to-four shift as he'd done for forty-five years. They had not had much to say to each other since Stephen had come.

"Your father's not much with words, y'know, Stephen," his mother had said.

Stephen had remembered. "That's not all," he said to his mother.

"Well, no, it's not all." His mother was apologetic. "He doesn't understand this woman taking her own life."

"I suppose he doesn't."

"Now I—you know sometimes, Stevie, things can get bad. I understand," his mother said. "But for your father, there is bad and good in the Bible and that was bad."

"Stephen, I come to say good-bye to you." It was Margaret's mother, Mrs. Steward.

"Good-bye, Mrs. Steward." He kissed her soft, plump cheek, fragile in retreat as baby's skin. "It is good of you to come round."

"I hope you'll not wait so long next time," she said. "I know it took you time to repair."

"I'll be back," he said. "Pia and I plan to come once a year."

"She's a nice girl, Pia. She could as well be your own girl. Ten years, remember?"

"I've thought about that."

"It's good you have her, Stephen. You won't be so lonely."

Kevin O'Malley from St. Mark's Eden Downs had a speech prepared, formal, predictable, sincere. He stood on the top step of Adine Williamson's house, read from the piece of paper he had written, eyes squinting in the unfamiliar sun, stumbling over words.

"Kevin, that was very kind," Stephen said to him afterwards. "It pleases me your memories of me here are better than my memories of myself."

"It would be good if you came back, Stephen," he said. "Especially after this great sadness you have had, one needs his home and family."

"It has been fine to come back, Kevin, and I'll come back again." Pia came up, put her arms around Stephen. "Here now, Kevin," he said. "Have you met my daughter?" Stephen asked. "This is Pia." His daughter. It had not come easily; it sounded out of place each time he said it.

Pia had disappeared the day that Emily died. Amos went with Stephen through the neighborhood to the homes of friends, to the school, finally to the police. When Stephen couldn't stand it any longer, Amos went alone.

He talked to the police with Charles and Margaret, who had arrived late in the afternoon. Stephen shut in solitude in the room he'd shared with Emily. He had never met Charles and Margaret. He didn't want to meet them now. Amos came in.

"I thought perhaps you didn't know," he said. "Emily made arrangements for you to have Pia."

"I didn't know," Stephen replied from the bed in the darkened room.

"Her brother, Charles, has a copy of a statement she made to a lawyer. He found it in her papers just now."

"I'm sure he's relieved," Stephen replied. "Please leave the light off."

"The police would like to talk with you."

"No."

"They simply want to know when you last saw Pia."

"You last saw Pia, Amos. When I came downstairs Pia had already left."

"All right," Amos said softly. "They also want to know whether you have any idea why Emily . . ."

"No."

"It's just for a report."

"I said I had no idea."

"All right."

"Amos?"

"Yes."

"That paper Charles Fielding found. Could I see it?"

Stephen put the paper on the desk under the lamp; he moved laboriously, with great effort and control;

turned on the lamp, pulled up a chair and sat with the paper in front of him, his head resting in his palms.

"Dated yesterday."

"So I see," Stephen replied.

It was written in Emily's hand on Harper and Harper stationery, dated November 11, 1966, signed by Emily, Mr. A. S. Harper and Annie Baxter—and stated simply:

> I would like to name Dr. Stephen Williamson as legal guardian of my daughter Pia Fielding.
>
> Emily Fielding

"It was intentional, then," Stephen said quietly. "Her dying."

"Not necessarily."

"You think it could have been an unbearable headache?" he asked. "She was having them."

"I know. Quite possibly," Amos replied. "Does it matter the circumstances?"

"Yes, it matters."

"We know too little. You'd been away, she only came to see me once. We know she took control at some point. She made arrangements for Pia."

"I can't believe that she had plans to die," Stephen said folding the paper, returning it to Amos. "Emily was brave."

"Yes, she was brave."

Charles knocked on the bedroom door.

"There're reporters."

"Reporters?" Stephen asked.

"For Laura Rand."

"Goddamn," he muttered. "I had forgotten Laura Rand. Of course there'd be reporters."

"I'll go," Amos said. "The light?"

"Turn it off." Stephen was back in bed.

"Amos?" he called after the older man. "You'll stay the night, won't you?"

"I'll stay."

On the floor beneath him, he could hear the reporters and the police. Occasionally Amos raised his voice and the telephone rang without ceasing. Surely he could not take Pia.

When Stephen awoke, it was dark and raining outside. The clock on Emily's dresser said 4:00 A.M.

He got up, turned on the light, went down to wake Amos about Pia.

"They are sure she's not gone," he said. "They think she may have gone to a friend's house. Someone she's close to."

Stephen needed something to do until morning, so he sorted through Emily's drawers. She had few clothes, and those she did have were old and faded, caked with clay, washed into the fabric or rich with oil paint. There were some letters, mainly from Cinderella, and mail from her television viewers stacked and tied by the year. Charles had written, and her father, Stephen's two recent letters from Chicago, the bills of sale from paintings she had sold, the reviews of her first showing, a picture of her when she was younger with someone else, ill fitting the frame. He looked more closely at the picture; the woman must have been Cinderella, a long, thin giant with arms like branches round the shoulders of Emily—and something in the brave stubbornness of Emily's face touched Stephen. He had loved her. He let go as he had never done when she was living—too careful with himself, afraid that giving might be losing, as though any loss could be equal to this.

"Amos," he called, racing down the stairs.

Amos was asleep again.

"We've got to find Pia."

"It's the middle of the night."

"It's nearly five."

"The police are looking, Stephen," he said. "Let's wait until seven."

Stephen did not wait. He went out on Pine Street in the rain and walked, walked until the rain had soaked through his trenchcoat and heavy sweater clear to his skin, walked all the way to his own apartment and then across Market Street and had a cup of coffee at the Deli. It was seven o'clock; the day was dark. At eight, when the town was thoroughly awake, he called Friends Select and asked for the address of a German boy new to the fifth grade.

The family of Gunther Schultz rented a row house in Center City, not far from Stephen. Mrs. Schultz answered the door. She was a large, distant German woman with a simple, rugged face; she spoke with a heavy accent and didn't let him in.

"I'm looking for Pia Fielding," he said. "She's in your son's class."

"Yes?"

"Her mother died," he said, "and she left her home yesterday after school."

"Who are you?"

"I am Stephen Williamson," he said. "Her father."

"You are Irish."

"Yes."

"She have no father," the woman said. "Once she told me that."

"I am her father now her mother's dead."

The German woman let him come inside. Breakfast dishes were piled in the sink and the kitchen smelled of bacon.

"Pia was good to my son, once," she said.

"Pia's very kind."

"Do you have coffee?"

Stephen took a cup.

"She will not eat."

"She is here?" Stephen asked.

The woman motioned with her head. "Up there," she said. "She will not talk. She is in the room at the back upstairs."

"Can I go up?"

The woman shrugged. "Why not?"

Pia sat in the corner of the bed, her legs drawn up and stared out at Stephen as he walked in and shut the door. He didn't speak to her. There were two beds in the room and he sat down on the bed next to Pia, his head away from her. He could hear her breathing, hesitant beside him, could hear the German woman in the kitchen washing up and the strident voice of a woman outside shouting at her child to do this or that or else she might not be able to do this and this and that. For a while, Pia didn't move.

"You're wet," she said at last.

"It's raining."

"I know." He heard her get up, her feet hit the floor and his bed yielded slightly beneath her weight.

"Have you been out all night?"

"Since five." He turned over on his back and faced her.

"How did you know to come here?"

"I just knew, that's all."

When they went downstairs, the German woman was sewing in the living room. She walked with them to the front door and gave Pia a small sack with an apple, a chicken leg and three cookies. Pia ate the cookies on the bus home.

"Good-bye," the German woman said, shaking hands with both of them solemnly. Stephen could see in her face that she'd known troubles.

"Good-bye," he said, put his cheek against hers. She was stiff but did not object.

That night after the arrangements had been made and the reporters seen to and the police and Amos Little had gone home and Pia finally sleeping in her own bed, Stephen burned the letter "To the Fielding Children" that Emily had given him to read. It made a bright yellow flame, tall above the sink where he burned it, then in seconds disintegrated, scattering its ashes around the white porcelain bowl.

For the next months, Stephen and Pia had gotten by daily, going about their separate business, taking no chances with each other. Then, in February, Stephen had said it was no good going on like this. Time had come for him to go home again—to come to terms with what he'd left behind and take Pia with him.

His father was coming home. Stephen saw him at a distance, the slanted gait, not tired, not resigned, old, perhaps, but somehow strong, approachable. The black lunch pail flapped against his slender thigh.

"So you are here yet," his father said.

"An hour more," Stephen replied. "Perhaps a little less."

"Here, let me wash up." His father walked into the cottage. "Then come off with me down the road."

"To the Headless Woman, Father?" Stephen asked, amused.

"Well?"

"Well."

"Once in a while a small drink doesn't hurt."

"Not a bit." Stephen laughed. "Once in a while, it helps a great deal."

There were the workers stopped in for a couple of drafts before going home to the regular business of evening; otherwise the Headless Woman was empty, and Stephen sat with his father in the back booth farthest away from the dart board.

"So you are going back to America?" his father said. Always he said the obvious—the uncontentionable.

"It's been a good trip."

"You ought to try it again sometime." Ron Williamson ordered another draft. "For a pain in the back," he retorted to Stephen's smile. "I find a lager does very well for a pain in the back."

"I thought it was Mother had pains in the back."

"Kidneys. Your mother has kidneys," Ron Williamson said. "I'm perfectly fit but creaky here and there." He clinked glasses. "To your safe return. And your next visit." He was a small, thin, wrinkled man who had always seemed since Stephen could remember to be sixty-five. "Your visits ought to be more frequent. Your mother isn't altogether well."

"You mentioned her kidneys."

"And her heart. There is no proof, but some indication."

"Pia and I will be back possibly at Christmas, at least a year from now."

His father rolled the glass mug back and forth in his hand in a thoughtful gesture, unspecific and uncharacteristic.

"There's something I've been meaning to inquire after," he began. Stephen suspected he had been composing this conversation for days as he sat on his stool in the factory pulling the lever, on the minute, taking out the faulty metal plates as they passed him on the conveyor belt, so familiar now, the faulty plates, the passing minute, that he could spend the eight hours save for lunch in the dignified world of his own mind, time for composing conversations, time for romance. Stephen wondered if his father knew about romance.

"I don't understand this woman who died and left you her child."

"No, I know you don't," Stephen said. "It has taken me time to come to a reckoning myself." He took out a small cigar, made a ceremony of lighting it. "It has something to do with what I've done these last three weeks—with coming home again. You've got to be able to come home and then you've got to be able to leave," he said carefully. "Emily went home, but she couldn't leave again. I suppose it drove her mad."

Ronald Williamson listened, but he didn't know what it was that Stephen said.

"It is difficult unless you were there, Father."

It had been difficult for Stephen. Once he had struggled through the rage and grief of Emily's dying, dark hours sitting in the solitude of his office, lying sleepless on Emily's bed at night, waking to empty sunless mornings, he had honestly believed he had died. Once that—there was still the question his father asked him now. It had come to him not suddenly, as he tried to have it come, as though a life's solution can be reduced to mathematic formula, but slowly, daily, without revelation, until one day he seemed to understand. When Emily fell in love with Stephen, it had touched the old wounds of her childhood, heretofore protected, when she had loved innocently and was betrayed. Vulnerable, she returned home, that cracking and degenerate fortress of her grandfather's, and bolted there by memory, she simply could not leave. It was not entirely satisfactory, but it seemed to make her dying inevitable and her living brave, as surely it had been.

Peter Williamson appeared in the pub door.

"Stephen," he shouted rudely, as was customary of him. "You'll have to stay in Belfast if you don't get a move on."

Stephen leaned over the table to his father.

"Simply, Ronald Williamson, I loved Emily and I love her daughter now."

"That is simple enough." Ron Williamson struggled

to his feet, looser at the joints than Stephen had seen him, and embraced his son there in public view, unlikely for this man of great reserve.

"Mother and Father want you home again soon," Peter said on the way to the airport. "They've plotted all these illnesses."

"So they've told me."

"Another thing, Stephen," Peter said. "Should you not get home for a while. There's a matter I want to settle with you. Before Albert died, he said all those books he bought, y'know the ones in the walnut bookcase that amount to quite a deal of money, he said they were for me. Now Rosie tells me she's going to leave them to you."

"When Rosie's dead, Peter, she won't know who'll be reading Albert's books now, will she?"

Peter smiled, slow to understand as he had always been since they were young, and then he laughed out loud.

"You're right, Stephen. She won't have the foggiest idea."

The plane lifted now over Belfast, past the city, over the bright green fields as carefully made as quilt patches. Out to sea.

"Wake up, Pia," Stephen said, jostling Pia sleeping against his arm. "We're leaving Ireland now. Watch so you'll remember it." Sleepy, Pia leaned across him, pressed her nose against the small window.

Once, early on after Emily's death when Stephen had been up all night with Pia rubbing her arms and legs and back and head because she couldn't sleep, he finally said in desperation to make her sleep, "What Emily Fielding was will be with us as long as we are alive, Pia. Especially with you, because she was your mother."

"D'you think so?" Pia had asked.

"I know so," he said and shortly she fell asleep.

Just on the shoreline as the land broke with the sea, there hovered a flock of gulls. Wings spread, bravely lingering over the sea. Then turning, as the wind turns, letting the wind carry them back to the shoreline, to the land.

SUSAN RICHARDS SHREVE

SUSAN RICHARDS SHREVE lives in Washington, D.C., with her husband and four children. Her first novel, *A Fortunate Madness,* was published in 1974.